Bitter, Sweet

LAURA BEST

NIMBUS
PUBLISHING

Nimbus Publishing Limited
PO Box 9166
Halifax, NS B3K 5M8
(902) 455-4286   www.nimbus.ca

Printed and bound in Canada

Design: Margaret Issenman
Author photo: Brian Best

This novel is a work of fiction. Names, characters, places, and incidents are either the product of the author's imagination or are used fictitiously. Any resemblance to actual persons, living or dead, events or locales is entirely coincidental.

Library and Archives Canada Cataloguing in Publication

        Best, Laura
        Bitter, sweet / Laura Best.
        ISBN 978-1-55109-736-7

I. Title.

PS8603.E777B58 2009   jC813'.6   C2009-903631-2

NOVA SCOTIA
Tourism, Culture and Heritage

Canadä

Canada Council | Le Conseil des Arts
for the Arts | du Canada

We acknowledge the financial support of the Government of Canada through the Book Publishing Industry Development Program (BPIDP) and the Canada Council, and of the Province of Nova Scotia through the Department of Tourism, Culture and Heritage for our publishing activities.

This book was printed on
Ancient-Forest Friendly paper

ANCIENT FOREST
FRIENDLY™

For my three M's
Melanie, Michelle, and Matt

Dalhousie Road
1948

Chapter One

That has to be the law, thought Pru Burbidge the day a strange car stopped in front of the house. It was late January and bitterly cold, even with a fire burning in the kitchen stove. The bottoms of all the windows were decorated with sheets of frost frozen so solid that Pru had just a small patch of glass to see through. An icy wind had whipped across the crest of the snow all that morning and shut the house completely off from the main road. Although a wide white expanse separated the house from the driver of the car, Pru was frightened. She wished Jesse were here. She had considered this exact situation many times in her mind, wondering what her reaction might be if the law came calling while she was home alone with Flora and Davey.

The car was sitting just a few feet past the row of maple trees and it might have been completely hidden had it not been for the fact that one of the trees had snapped in two during a big windstorm late last summer and had needed to be removed.

❊ ❊ ❊

Reese Buchanan helped Jesse cut the tree up for firewood—they worked all day cutting and splitting. The air was cool and a light breeze rustled through the treetops. Mama said it was perfect wood-splitting weather and it couldn't have been more perfect for working than if they had ordered the weather up special. Then she said they would have to celebrate the firewood later when she was feeling less tired.

"Reese has been a good friend to us, Pru," Mama said as she sat beside the window watching them work up the wood. "I don't know what we would have done way out here in Dalhousie without him."

Reese stayed for supper and Mama sat at the table with her housecoat wrapped around her because she didn't feel up to getting properly dressed. She kept thanking Reese, and Reese kept saying, "Oh, it was really nothing," looking more bashful each time.

❋ ❋ ❋

For a time no one got out of the car, but it made Pru nervous all the same. Pulling the curtain back just far enough to get a clear view without being seen, Pru gestured for Flora and Davey to keep quiet. The two youngest Burbidges were playing a game of go fish, laughing whenever one of them called for a card that the other was holding. Reese had brought the deck of cards over last week. They were old and worn and twice their normal thickness, but every queen and king and ace was accounted for. The cards had been a great distraction, and with the all the snow outside and not being able to make it out to the schoolhouse most days, they'd spent much of their time shuffling the deck of cards back and forth.

Davey laid his cards down and joined his older sister at the window, stretching up on his tiptoes to see out. "Who's that, Pru?" he asked, as if sensing her apprehension.

"It might be the law or someone from Children's Aid," she said, knowing that both were equally serious.

"The law?"

"Take Flora and go upstairs," said Pru in her most authoritative voice, the one that she'd been practising since Mama got sick.

"Come on, Flora," said Davey, not bothering to argue with Pru, which his older sister was most grateful for.

"You be quiet as mice. And watch out for that broken step!" Pru called out as she heard them shuffle up the stairs. There was a small cubbyhole at the top of the staircase beneath the attic steps; this was the place they were supposed to hide if ever they were told to, the place both Pru and Jesse knew they could fit in as well. There was a small latch on the inside of the door that could be hooked if need be. Pru had always hoped that need would not arise.

Pru had no reason to believe that the police had been sent for them, but it had been the first thing that came into her mind when she saw the strange car parked out by the road. Besides, Mama had warned them that this might happen.

"You be careful what you tell them," Mama had said. "Don't tell them any more than they want to know. And no matter what, don't look like you've got something to hide. They'll send you all away and that'll be the last you'll see of one another. You'll end up in foster homes or at the orphan house."

Pru knew her brothers and sister looked up to her; all of them did, including Jesse, even though he was the oldest. Jesse rarely made any important decision without first consulting her. But they had decided it would have to be that way right from the start. *A united front.* Mama had said that the most important thing was that they stick together.

"There'll be times when you might not agree," Mama had said, looking up at them from her sick bed. "But you stick together all the same. If you want to keep the family together you have to form a united front."

Only now there was a strange car parked out by the road and Jesse was not there for Pru to consult. He was gone into town with Reese Buchanan to cash Mama's government cheque and buy some food. They had only been gone an hour or so and were not likely to return anytime soon.

Pru stood at the window, nervously watching to see if

someone was going to get out of the car. One set of tracks, which belonged to Jesse, created a narrow winding path from the house to the road. It had started to blow shut, and was barely visible now. Jesse thought not shovelling the drive was a good way to keep people away. The last thing they needed was some stranger poking around, asking nosey questions. Pru wondered if the stranger in the parked car would wade through the deep snow, and if he did, what his reasons would be for doing so.

"Go away, go away," whispered Pru, rocking gently back and forth as she stood by the window. But she was not so lucky. The car door opened and although the snow on the ground and hanging on the trees muffled the sounds from outside, it did not silence the thump of the car door as it closed.

The first morning after the storm the house had felt safe and snug heaped up with snow, something Pru hadn't felt for months. Were it not for the sound of Jesse already out of bed and rattling the lids on the wood stove, she might have allowed herself the small indulgence of lying in bed a bit longer, savouring the crisp quietness that lay beyond her bedroom window. She might have imagined herself sailing across the sparkling white waves of snow, off to some exotic land in search of adventure.

But now the house no longer gave Pru a sense of security. Now the mounds of snow and the heavily cloaked trees filled her with a feeling of entrapment. How would they escape if the man approaching her door was the law? Where would they run to?

Pru waited for the soft thump of boots on the doorstep.

Chapter Two

Time stood still as Pru waited for the stranger to walk up the path to the house, to tread upon the weatherworn steps that led to her front door, to pound on the door or rattle the latch. So strong was her fear in those moments of waiting that her own heartbeat drowned out the sound of the wind wailing outside the door. What would she say? More importantly, what would this person want?

Strangers did not visit their house. There had to be some reason for this man to be wading through the snow toward them. Mrs. McFarland from up the road used to drop in just to be nosey, but she had since stopped visiting, and sometimes the people from Red Cross would stop by, but they had already been to the house in December to make their delivery of winter coats and were not likely to drop by again anytime soon.

Last summer the local reverend had come by to visit them and had ended up staying for hours. "War is a terrible thing, Mrs. Burbidge," he'd said to Mama. "Lives lost, families torn apart. The country is still reeling from the effects and will be for some time to come. Bodies can be mended but spiritual needs are often overlooked."

The reverend had continued his spiel about the horrors of war and the need for people to turn toward the church for solace, ending with an invitation for the Burbidges to join the congregation some Sunday. "And the choir is in dire need of a few good singers," he'd added with a wink.

Mama had smiled and said, "We'll have to see." Only that was Mama's polite way of saying no.

※ ※ ※

Mama invited the reverend to stay for supper and sent Pru out to the garden to pick some peas and beans. Jesse stoked up the fire even though it had been far too warm for one. Still, the reverend was a guest in their home and it would have hardly been fitting to dish up a cold supper. Besides, there was little else that could have been served on such short notice.

The reverend sat out on the front verandah and helped Pru and Mama shell the peas. Pru worried that Mama would get one of her nosebleeds, but she didn't. Mama didn't do much talking and neither did the reverend.

Pru felt too awkward in the reverend's presence to do anything other than what Mama instructed her to. She had cooked hodgepodge before; in fact, she made all the meals, even on those days when Mama felt a bit better. It was good practice for Pru, and she knew that the day was fast approaching when Mama wouldn't be there for her to ask how to prepare this or that.

Mama was apologetic—there wasn't any cream for the hodgepodge. "Hodgepodge without cream is hardly hodgepodge at all," she said.

"Our Lord was served but bread and fish, if I recall," the reverend replied as Pru set the steaming pot in the centre of the table.

"You're only being kind," said Mama.

After the reverend offered up grace—something that had never once happened at their table before—he ate as though it were a meal fit for a king. Flora and Davey watched him with curiosity, their usual mealtime antics forgotten for the time being even though the reverend made no attempts to put on airs. He smacked his food and slurped his tea just like you'd expect a regular person would. Pru even saw him wipe his chin with his coat sleeve.

The two youngest Burbidges knew little about manners nor did they care to and Mama could not seem to bring herself to correct them when they were at the table. In fact, she couldn't bring herself to correct any of their behaviour since her illness. The way Pru saw it, the reverend fit in quite nicely at their table, even in all his holiness, although it didn't cause her to trust him any more. He was still, after all, a stranger to them, regardless of his outward behaviour or the fact that he got to talk to God on a regular basis and, Pru figured, he was quite likely responsible for at least the occasional miracle being performed on His behalf. When the reverend spoke, God listened, of that Pru had no doubt.

"Very fine, Mrs. Burbidge," the reverend said. "This is all very fine. My compliments to the young cook." He smiled and nodded in Pru's direction.

"Pru is cook of the family," Mama said proudly. "And Jesse is the fire keeper. Davey is the storyteller. And Flora—" She stopped to pause for a brief time, "Flora is the darling of us all."

"Amen to that," Jesse said, setting his empty plate on the sideboard. Pru could tell that this little declaration had pleased Mama. It was as genuine and clean as the opening of the morning glories that twined around the verandah posts, and it was said without time for him to be thinking of something just to impress the reverend.

※ ※ ※

The Burbidges were not church-goers, although Mama had sometimes brought God's name up, and not just when she was good and mad like when Daddy up and left. After Mama had gotten sick she'd stopped getting mad. She just smiled whenever something went wrong and said that if they waited a few moments something better would come along, and it usually did. If it didn't, Mama would say it obviously wasn't meant to be.

Pru often thought of the day the reverend came for supper. How Mama had been wearing her pretty red and gold dress, the only good dress she owned. How it had saddened her to see Mama come out of the bedroom wearing it, the way the fabric hung in such an unattractive way on her body. Mama had worn that same dress the day they all took the train to Annapolis to visit Nanny Gordon. Nanny Gordon had come running out of the house to greet them and had placed her hands on Mama's waist. "Why, just look at you, Issy," she'd said, laughing aloud, "as plump and round as a dumpling!"

※ ※ ※

The wind let out a mighty blast that shook the entire house. Pru jumped like a scared rabbit. Just as she expected to hear the sound of boots plodding up the snow-covered steps or a knock at the door, the floorboards above her creaked.

"Pru…Pru! It's dark and I'm tired," came Flora's small squeaky voice.

"Hello?" came a muffled cry from outside in the snow. "Hello in there!"

Pru stood frozen in her tracks in the middle of the living room. Perhaps whoever it was would go away if she did nothing at all.

"Pru…" implored Flora. "Davey says there's a rat."

Of all things! Couldn't Davey behave himself just this once?

"Quiet!" Pru warned as harshly as she could without raising her voice.

"I know there's someone in there. I can see the smoke coming out of the chimney." The voice paused for a moment then continued. "Can you come to the door at least?"

"Pru…."

Pru spun around and ran to the bottom of the stairs. "The only rat up there is you, David Burbidge," she said harshly. "Now stop pestering Flora this minute. You stop it and you be quiet. Remember what Mama told you."

Not another sound came from upstairs, although Pru could clearly hear Flora climbing back into the cubbyhole beneath the attic steps.

Pru grabbed her coat and slowly pried open the front door. A man dressed from head in toe in winter clothes was standing on the ground below the steps. When he removed his cap, Pru recognized him as Mr. Dixon, the man who had helped Mama get her government cheques coming once they figured out that Daddy wasn't coming home.

"What can I do for you, Mr. Dixon?" she asked, shoving her arms into her coat sleeves. She hoped he would not hear the slight quiver in her voice.

"I won't come any farther in case I'm carrying some germs. There's been an outbreak of influenza. Whole families quarantined," said Mr. Dixon. "I didn't see much of a path to the road. Is everyone in the house all right?"

"We're all feeling fine. Jesse's gone into town with Reese Buchanan but he'll shovel us out when he gets back." The wind tugged at Pru's coat as she held it shut.

"How's Isadora these days?"

"Mama's doing fine, too," said Pru. "She's busy or she would have come to the door herself."

"Her cheques are coming regularly?"

"Every month."

"And the baby bonus, too?"

Pru nodded.

"That's good, then. Really good. It's hardly a woman's fault when her man takes off like that," said Mr. Dixon, pulling his cap back on. "If you need anything, you tell your mama to let me know. That's what your councillor's for, to work for the people, help them out when they need helping." He was still talking as he trudged back through the snow to his car. Pru thought he sounded as if he were hot on the campaign trail.

Pru stepped back inside and closed the door. She did not know if she was trembling from the cold or the sense of relief that was surging through her.

Chapter Three

After she died, we buried Mama behind the house. Jesse dug a narrow grave in the spot Mama had showed him two weeks earlier, not far from the little tombstone that read:

JOHN MARSH
SON OF ELIJAH AND MARY
1862–1863

There were three tombstones behind the house, all in line and set inside an old wooden fence. When we first moved in, Reese told us that a lot of houses in Dalhousie had these tiny cemeteries from before the churches were built.

❋ ❋ ❋

Jesse and I wrapped Mama in that Dutch girl quilt she kept on her bed. We shut the door because we didn't want Davey and Flora to see what we were doing. We moved the quilt about the bed real gentle-like, tucking it all around and folding the bottom up around Mama's feet, because we had never done something like this before and we were not at all sure how we should proceed. The thought never crossed my mind that Mama shouldn't have died, because Mama always said that there are no mistakes, just hurdles we have to get over, and that we all do what we have to in order to make it over those hurdles.

"Should we leave her slippers on?" I asked, but Jesse did not answer. Instead he began folding the quilt around Mama's feet. I knew that Mama would say it was a darn shame to be burying her slippers like that when surely someone else could get some use from them.

※ ※ ※

The slippers were new—well, not really new, but new to Mama. We bought them at a rummage sale one day when Reese Buchanan took me and Flora into town. Once we counted up the change we had there wasn't quite enough, so Reese chipped in a nickel. "They'll look real nice on Isadora," he said.

They looked like ballerina slippers, and for a brief moment I pretended that they were magical and perhaps had the power to make Mama well again. It was a silly thing to pretend, but Mama always said that some days it was hard enough to live with what is, let alone ignoring what could be.

Mama slid the pink slippers on her bare feet, giggling like a young girl and clicking her feet together. "We should celebrate," she said. "It's not every day a woman gets a pair of fancy pink slippers to wear."

So we all dressed up in silly getups—Davey wearing one of Mama's pots on his head and spinning the broomstick around and around like a baton, Flora with a sheet wrapped around her body, calling herself the Queen of Sheba and making movements like she was belly dancing as she performed for Mama. Jesse put on one of Mama's dresses and tied an apron around his head, and I wore a pair of pants and a shirt and stuck some old hay in under a straw hat.

Before we put on the parade that day, Jesse took a piece of coal from the firebox and we all blackened out our front teeth. We had so much fun as we rubbed the black coal on our teeth. I don't know why making out that we didn't have any teeth seemed so funny to us, because most of Mama's teeth were rotted down to stubs. Why she did not suffer toothaches all the while she was sick I could not for the life of me figure out. Many nights, after hearing her walk the floor, I'd climb out of bed and find her holding a warm towel to her jaw. But that was before she got the sickness.

"Kiss me, darling," Flora said, removing the sheet from her mouth and giving us a black toothy smile.

"Who's doing all the laughing?" Mama called from her bedroom.

"It's only the woodland fairies!" Davey hollered back from outside her bedroom door while we tried our best to stifle our laughs without smudging coal all over our face and hands.

"Well then, fairies," Mama said with a slight air of indignation, "you'd best go back to Fairyland before my children come home and find you in their place. They are the best children in the world and can't be replaced, even by magical woodland fairies." Hearing the sweet musical sound in her voice filled my heart with joy.

"Not until we sprinkle the house with fairy dust for good luck," Davey replied, smiling at all of us as he clowned around with Mama.

"Sprinkle it quickly," said Mama, "because I'm about as far out of luck as I can get. Sprinkle it and then go back to that hollow stump in the woods where you live."

※ ※ ※

Mama and Davey shared many secrets about the fairies. Mama said that with her being Irish it was only natural for her to believe. But she also said that Gran Hannah, her grandmother on her father's side, was of Mi'kmaq decent and had sometimes spoken of the little people as well, so she'd gotten a double dose of it.

Mama believed that Gran Hannah had possessed some kind of special powers. There were many things that Mama saw and heard while growing up that made her think this way. She could remember waking up one morning with Gran Hannah bedside her in bed. Gran Hannah's arms were folded across her chest and her eyes were wide open, but when Mama called out to her she would not wake up. Thinking she had died through the night, Mama ran to get her mother, but when they returned Gran Hannah was just getting up, stretching and yawning as if waking from a peaceful sleep.

"What was wrong with you?" Mama asked her.

"I went on a little trip," Gran Hannah said, smiling, "to see my ancestors, the old men and women who were here first. They are waiting to gather us all up when we die."

Mama said she knew that Gran Hannah was not of this world as she lay on the bed. "She had no breath," Mama said firmly. "She came back from the dead. She had to have."

Mama watched Gran Hannah with suspicion for years afterward, not knowing why, only that she felt some need to learn the truth about who her grandmother really was. Gran Hannah died before Mama ever found out that truth, but not before she had passed on many of her secrets.

Sometimes when the wind whistled in around the windows at night, Mama would crawl up on the bed beside me, pull the curtain back, and peek out into the darkness. "Do you hear that?" she'd ask, smiling as she tapped on the windowpane. "That's Gran Hannah whistling at us."

❋ ❋ ❋

Davey knocked on the door and asked Mama if she was ready. Jesse and I were as excited as Flora and Davey, giggling and tittering, trying to keep our lips from covering our teeth and at the same time not wanting the coal to mix with our saliva and make a horrible taste in our mouths.

"Ready, willing, and waiting," Mama answered.

Flora pushed open the bedroom door. Mama was sitting up on top of the bed with her pretty pink slippers displayed on top of a little white pillow like they were valuable artifacts from a museum.

"Presenting…" Davey said in his best master of ceremonies voice, "for your very own entertainment…the Burbidge tribe!" Mama laughed at his choice of words to describe her children, secretly pleased of her Mi'kmaq lineage even though her own father had been ashamed to admit it. We spent that rainy afternoon entertaining Mama in her bedroom, celebrating the pink slippers and the fact that she was there to wear them. Mama always liked to find some reason to celebrate because, she said, it sure beat crying your heart out over things you had no control over. Mama could find reasons to celebrate most anything. She said that celebrating was the same as counting your blessing out loud, really loud. She also said that we'd be more likely to remember a celebration than some whispered thank you we made to our Father in heaven at the supper table or while bent down at the foot of our beds.

And, as usual, Mama was right. I couldn't think of a single thing to be thankful for while we were wrapping Mama in the quilt, but I could remember the smile on her face each time we had a celebration.

❉ ❉ ❉

Mama said a coffin was too expensive, not to mention that there would be too many questions asked if we tried to get one. The last thing Mama wanted was for anyone, especially the government, to know our family business. Instead, she told us to just wrap her in that quilt.

"It's a pretty enough quilt," she said.

But shortly after Mama closed her eyes for the last time, Jesse had a better idea. He scrounged up some lumber from the walls of the rundown old pig house and nailed the boards together.

"Do you think Mama will mind, Pru?" he asked.

"I bet she wouldn't mind one bit," I said.

Mama had planned everything out just right—even her sickness—because she hadn't wanted Flora and Davey to be afraid once it came time to do everything. She'd spent as much time talking about her death as she did planning out how we were to survive once God took her back with him.

Jesse dug the hole that night beneath the light of the full moon and later he said it was as if it was meant to happen when it did, the way the moon had given him just enough light to work by. Except what Jesse didn't know was that Mama had planned it all out herself, made sure it happened when she'd wanted it to. Jesse didn't know but I did and I also knew I would never tell.

Jesse kept jabbering away after he came in from digging

and I imagined that the moon had somehow gotten into him and it was building itself up into a huge combustible ball right in the centre of him. His eyes had grown in size, and his pupils had opened up like deep dark holes. I knew Jesse had been looking to me to agree with him, to tell him that yes, everything did seem to be just right, but I'd been too numb, my brain crammed full from trying to remember all the last-minute things that Mama had told me those final few weeks when she was living.

We buried Mama early in the morning, before the sun had time to push its golden head up over the earth. Jesse and I should have felt guilty for making the little ones get up from their beds at that hour when they had only fallen asleep a few short hours before, but Jesse said we couldn't risk someone coming by. He said the morning was the best time. I could see the logic in what he was saying. Besides, when Mama was alive and well she'd sit and wait for the sun to bring a start to another day, so that part seemed right.

I read from the Bible because Flora and Davey thought Mama wouldn't go to heaven if I didn't. I read the part about there being a time and a purpose for everything, which I thought seemed fitting considering everything Mama had gone through that last while. Davey and Flora cried while I tried to make my voice sound strong. Mama would be counting on me. I couldn't let her down.

Chapter Four

Mrs. McFarland was the one who told Mama about the baby bonus and the fact that she'd have to make sure we were registered for school in order to get her fair share of the money the government was sending out.

"Just fill out the form and those cheques are as good as in the mail. Right up 'til they're sixteen," said Mrs. McFarland. "It's kind of like finding a gold mine."

"It might help to keep some of them in school," said Mama.

"Almost makes a person feel like having more." Mrs. McFarland let out a girlish laugh. Mama laughed politely and said she was more than satisfied with the family she had.

"What's she doing here all the time?" Jesse asked, which wasn't at all fair considering that company never showed up at our door, except for Reese Buchanan. And it wasn't as if Mrs. McFarland was there all that often, at least not in the beginning. "And I'm not a baby," Jesse said, folding his arms at his chest. "So what's all this talk about baby bonuses?"

Mama smiled and said, "They have to call it something.

And if it's free money coming from the government they can call it whatever they please."

"It's not free," said Jesse. "I've got to go to school."

※ ※ ※

We were all sent off to school for the very first time that fall, each of us carrying a lard kettle packed with bread and molasses. Flora had her red hair done up in pigtails, which were held in place by rubber jar rings that were too old and worn for canning. It was all Mama had to fasten them in place, and Flora had her heart set on pigtails for that first day. The pigtails flipped and flopped whenever Flora shook her head, which was often, as she liked the way they felt swishing back and forth. Davey was excited about going to school, but then again, Davey liked going any place so long as he was on the move. It didn't seem to bother him that he had to get up each morning and wash his hands and face before leaving the house. Jesse walked all grumpy the first day, kicking his lard kettle down the dirt road all the way to school. I expected the lid to come flying off and his bread and molasses to end up strewn in the dirt, but it didn't. I think Jesse almost expected it as well, as he seemed to kick it with more spite the closer we got to the schoolhouse.

I could scarcely contain the excitement I felt at knowing I'd soon be reading and writing and learning more things than I ever thought imaginable. There were so many things I longed to know, so many strange places in the world to learn about, it hardly seemed possible. But the moment I stepped over the threshold and into the schoolhouse I wanted to turn around and run for home. There was scarcely a face I recognized in the crowd. I saw two girls whispering in the corner and thought they must be talking about me: Pru Burbidge, the nobody girl, the girl who arrived at school carrying her lard kettle without a scribbler or pencil in sight.

Most of the children arrived that first day carrying their supplies—wooden pencil boxes, thick white notebooks without a single word messing up the pages—and I envied the way they seemed to belong inside those four walls when it was obvious to me, and everyone else, that the Burbidges did not fit in at all. Miss Pinkham, our teacher, made a list of the things we'd need for school. I dreaded the thought of showing Mama the list, knowing that these things would not be free, but she did not grumble when she saw the list. Instead she asked Reese to take her to town the next day to pick up what we needed.

You get used to seeing what other kids have, like the big box of crayons Celia Trask carried to and from school every day even though Miss Pinkham said there was no need to bring that big box of crayons every day since we only had the one day set aside for being creative. Miss Pinkham had her own box of crayons and when it came time for us to colour she would share them amongst those of us who had no crayons of our own. Each time she'd draw three or four crayons from her box I would hold my breath, hoping that she'd give me the gold crayon, the only colour in the box I ever hoped for. I wanted to colour everything gold and make it worth a million dollars. The gold crayon could make us rich, I thought. If only I could get my fingers on it.

Amos Dory was the only one at school with an honest-to-goodness lunch box, which we were told had been sent to him by his uncle in Massachusetts. How I coveted that shiny red metal box sitting on his desk. I thought it sparkled like nothing I had ever seen before. I wanted to pick it up in my hand and let it swing freely at the end of my arm as I walked to school. I wanted to have everyone see me arriving and whisper how lucky I was. I convinced myself that if I could only touch it, run my fingers across its cool shiny surface, I would be happy. But Amos did not look like the friendly type. I knew that making this small request to him was not likely to get me any closer to my goal and would more than likely make me the brunt of cruel jokes.

Poor Pru Burbidge can't get her hands on Amos Dory's lunch kettle. Poor, poor Pru Burbidge.

Miss Pinkham would wait until we had eaten our lunches before going home for her own, secure in the knowledge that we were all safe to play on our own outside until she returned. Some days she would put Celia Trask in charge of us, other days she would assign the task to Philip Jelly so that no one could accuse her of playing favourites.

One day I waited until everyone else had gone outside and then took Amos's red lunch kettle down from the shelf and held it close to my chest. The handles were still warm from Amos's touch and the core from the Gravenstein apple he'd eaten at noon was still giving off a mouth-watering smell.

I remembered the apple trees lined up in Basil Dory's orchard the previous summer, laden with green apples, and how Jesse had run through the ditch and pulled off handfuls of apples and brought them out to the road for the rest of us. We'd run back home, sat down beneath our own barren apple tree, and devoured them all. Their tartness had sent my back teeth aching but I continued to bite and chew until their taste became bearable. Late that night I woke with pains in my stomach. I pulled my knees close to my chest and hoped they would pass quickly, wondering how something so deplorable could transform itself into something so mouth-watering in only a few short weeks.

My stomach growled as I held the lunch kettle in my hands. The bread and molasses sandwich I'd eaten for lunch had not satisfied my hunger. I opened the lunch box quickly to get a better smell. One smell. That's all I wanted. It seemed like such a simple thing. I only wish Celia Trask had felt the same way.

"Thief. Thief!" Celia cried out the second I opened the lunch kettle. For the life of me, I could not figure out what she was talking about or to whom she was yelling.

"You there, Pru Burbidge!" I spun around.

A rush of footsteps pounded across the small porch. Everyone in the school had congregated at the door and they were all looking at me. Amos Dory navigated his way through the crowd, his feet thumping against the floor as he crossed the room toward me. I cowered as he drew near. He removed the shiny red lunch kettle from my hands, peeked inside, and pulled out a second apple.

"You could have asked." He dropped the apple in my hand and returned outside to play, calling the crowd of students out with him.

I was left standing there with the apple in my open palm. Jesse, Flora, and Davey stood in the doorway, looking at me as if they couldn't quite believe what they were seeing.

"I was just looking at his lunch kettle," I explained. "I didn't even know he had an apple." I heard Jesse swear beneath his breath before he walked out the door.

The next day there was another apple sitting on my desk, and each morning after that. I would take the apples home and cut them into pieces to share with Flora and Davey. Jesse wanted no part in the "pity food," as he called it, but I was too much of a little pig to care.

❋ ❋ ❋

Mama thought our going to school was a fair enough trade and said it pretty much amounted to us getting paid to learn even with the inconvenience of having to find something every day to put in our lard kettles for lunch. Once the government knew we were all signed up for school the first cheque came to the post office. The welfare money Mr. Dixon had secured for Mama had sometimes run out before the end of the month, but now the government was paying Mama baby bonuses of five dollars for Flora, six dollars for Davey, and eight dollars each for Jesse and me, which amounted to even more than Mama's welfare cheque. We were suddenly made rich, at least by our standards.

Mama twirled herself around in the kitchen the day that first baby bonus cheque came. Kissing that little brown envelope, she kicked up her heels like a spring colt. Her dress flared out from her body like she was square dancing and being tossed about by an invisible partner. She nearly knocked into the kitchen table before she stopped.

"Things are looking up for the Burbidges!" she said, whooping in a way I'd never heard her do before. Of course we all whooped and hollered too. Then she walked down to Mrs. Hurley's store with all four of us in tow, smiling back at us from time to time.

We stood in the doorway, unable to believe what was happening, as Mama told Mrs. Hurley to count out some peppermint candies in a small paper bag. Mama ignored Mrs. Hurley when she said, "Some would say it's not right for the county to be paying for such unnecessary indulgences."

Even Mrs. Hurley's sour comments could not dampen Mama's spirits that day, and for the first time in a long time I remembered what it felt like to be able to buy something that wasn't absolutely needed. It almost made up for me not having a bright shiny new lunch kettle or a big box of crayons with so many different colours you knew you'd never get the chance to use them all.

We didn't waste the candies. Mama set them out on the table when we got home and doled them out into four piles. When Jesse saw that Mama didn't keep any for herself, he insisted that she take her share. We all had to sing out that it was only fair and true for her to share in our good fortune before she collected them up from the table.

"I really shouldn't," she said. "Oh, the toothache I'll get."

"Eat them one at a time, Mama," Flora said, her cheek bulging as she held a peppermint in her mouth. This sent us all into a fit of laughter. Flora could not for the life of her understand what was so funny. The truth of it was that we'd have laughed at anything Flora said since we were all stirred by our imaginations over what all this extra money would mean. We didn't know then how quickly our happiness would be pulled out from under us.

※ ※ ※

When Mama got sick, Mrs. McFarland started coming by every week, some days staying until we got home from school. She cleaned all the corners of the house and mixed up bread for us to eat and wasn't the least bit backwards when it came to asking Mama questions like did she think Daddy would ever come back?

"When pigs fly," Mama would answer with a rigid jaw.

I knew that Mama wasn't about to have Mrs. McFarland take pity on her just because Daddy hadn't come home from working in the tobacco fields. By this time it had been nearly a year since he'd left and it hardly seemed possible that he was planning on coming back. Flora would sometimes cry after Mrs. McFarland left. I think it made her miss Daddy even more the way Mrs. McFarland was always asking about him. Mama said no one should have to put up with the likes of Emily McFarland and her "none-of-your-business" questions.

Sometimes Mama would lie down and rest while Mrs. McFarland worked, but that wouldn't stop Mrs. McFarland from talking to Mama through the open bedroom door. Other times Mama felt up to sitting in the rocking chair or even sweeping the floor or washing dishes. Later, she would chide herself over some of the things she'd told Mrs. McFarland without meaning to.

"She's like a dog with a bone. Never happy until you tell her something. And the questions she can come up with," said Mama, shaking her head. "I don't know what you'd have to tell her to keep her satisfied."

"She's got no business asking anything," said Jesse. "Tell her to get lost. Tell her we don't want her help."

"She'll get tired of this eventually," Mama told us as she stood by the window one day watching Mrs. McFarland walk down the driveway on her way home. But a few weeks turned into a month, and still Mrs. McFarland made her rounds. Then one day she started telling Mama over and over that it was time she should see a doctor.

"I'm not sick. I'm just tired," Mama would say, smiling like Mrs. McFarland was forcing some good health on her. But we could all see the dark lines beneath her eyes, the hours she spent sleeping only to awaken tired. And then one day Mama fell on her way upstairs. Her foot went through a rotten floorboard on the sixth step. We helped her to her bed and Jesse fixed the broken board as best he could but he had very little to work with and could not do a proper job.

"Out back near the well, the yarrow is rich and high—go pick some, Pru," Mama said, looking up at me from the bed, her face drained of its colour.

"What's it for, Mama?" asked Flora, giving Mama a peculiar look.

"Pru knows," said Mama, flashing me a knowing look. It pleased me to know that Mama had so much faith in me, even though I had never yet had reason to use any of Gran Hannah's remedies, and even though I wasn't altogether sure I would do it right.

So I did as Mama asked, spurred by a sense of urgency—already I could see a swelling beginning to fester in her ankle. I pounded the yarrow leaves to a pulp and placed the compress on her ankle and hoped for the best.

"You're learning, Pru," said Mama. "This is good practice for you. In the morning I'll be good as new."

"I wish I didn't need to practise anything at all," I said, a gnawing feeling growing inside me—a feeling that everything would not be good as new the way Mama had predicted.

The next day Mama's ankle was black and blue. Her leg was black and blue as well. She was always black and blue after that, each time some new place. Every time it happened Mrs. McFarland would *tut-tut* over it, telling Mama to take herself to the doctor.

Mama didn't know how else to make Mrs. McFarland go away, so one day she had Reese Buchanan drive her to a doctor she didn't know in Bridgewater. She called it assurance.

"I want to be sure the doctor doesn't know who I am. People have big enough mouths as it is and the worst of it is they never get the story straight. At least this'll put an end to Emily McFarland harping at me all the time." There was a slight hesitancy in her voice when she said this. I think even then Mama had some inkling of what was to come.

After Mama's trip to the doctor I had to learn to sign her name on the government cheques, even though it felt wrong to be doing it. And Mama said we had to get rid of Mrs. McFarland. We had to stop her from coming to the house.

Chapter Five

Mama told Mrs. McFarland that her blood was low and the doctor had put her on iron pills. "The silly little things that can go wrong with a person's body," she said, tossing her mane of auburn hair.

"I'm not surprised," said Mrs. McFarland. "It's all part of the curse, you know."

"What curse?" Flora asked.

"Why, the curse of being a woman, child. But you'll find that out someday," she said, reaching beneath her flabby chin for her coat button. She removed her coat and hung it on the door, on the same nail Daddy used to hang his jacket, and went for the broom.

"Pru just swept the floor," Mama said, stopping Mrs. McFarland before she made it to the corner of the kitchen where the broom stood.

"Why, you darling, thoughtful girl. You're growing into quite a young lady," said Mrs. McFarland, beaming a smile so bright and shiny at me that I dreaded the thought of what was to come. I imagined her hauling her dress up above her knee, heaving one leg over the broomstick, and flying out through the open door, cackling like the witch I thought her to be. Except I knew it would not be so easy. I knew that even if Mrs. McFarland possessed special powers like that she was not about to take her leave without a great deal of resistance.

Maybe Mama thought the same thing too, because then she said something that made Mrs. McFarland furious. She told her there was no need of her coming by and doing her work for her.

"As soon as my iron is built up I'll be fine. So I don't see any reason for you to be doing what you're doing. Besides, Pru is a big enough help now. She's capable of doing most everything." Mama's voice was deadly serious. She was looking directly at Mrs. McFarland, and there wasn't a sign of a smile on her face.

"She can't mix bread," said Mrs. McFarland, all red-faced like someone had just slapped her hard on the cheeks.

"But she'll learn."

Mama continued to speak softly but firmly, with a clear determination that this was the way she wanted it—with no butting in from Mrs. McFarland. The house became incredibly calm, like the quiet of the leaves right before the rain comes pouring down.

"Of all the ungrateful…of all the ungrateful…" Mrs. McFarland's mouth opened up like a trap door. She pulled her coat off the back of the door and shoved her arms in the sleeves. As she fastened her coat, that double chin of hers quivered like the wattles on a turkey gobbler's neck.

"She can't mix bread. Pru can't mix bread," I heard her say as she hurried for the door. But when she reached the door she turned around with spite. "Some day you'll wish you hadn't turned down my help, Isadora Burbidge. It might be too late then."

Mrs. McFarland marched down the steps, her arms moving mightily back and forth as if she was pounding the air. Mama didn't say a word as she watched her walk away for the last time.

"I could write Tom," said Mama, as if thinking aloud, once Mrs. McFarland was out of sight.

"No! Not Uncle Tom," Jesse cried out. "Not after what he did to you, Mama. To all of us."

Mama looked up at Jesse in surprise. "You call on family when you need to," she said.

"Family!" exclaimed Jesse. "Daddy always said family's the worst—they'll steal the eyes right out of your head if you give them the chance."

"Well, Daddy didn't know everything!" Mama cried back.

Jesse stormed from the house, the door rattling in his wake.

Tears formed in Mama's eyes as she pulled out her tablet and began to write. "Sometimes you have to swallow your pride, Pru. It's time Jesse learned that."

※ ※ ※

Right before Christmas the people from Red Cross showed up at our door with winter coats. This did not come as any surprise, as they had done so the year before. I hated walking into the schoolhouse wearing the Red Cross coats for the first time because I thought everyone could tell they were welfare coats, given to us because otherwise we would not have had a thing fit to wear in public.

Willie Thompson would sometimes come to school without a coat on at all, except he lived right across from the schoolhouse and no one dared to laugh or make fun of him. Not big Willie Thompson, who didn't give a fig if he learned or not as long as his mother got her monthly cheque. And he sure didn't mind telling Miss Pinkham this, either. No sir, not Willie. There was nothing backwards or shy about the way he'd rest his head on his desk after lunch and have himself a little snooze.

In the beginning Miss Pinkham would try and rouse him from his sleep. He'd pick his head up from his desk and say, "I just got to be here, Miss Pinkham. Government can't make me learn."

All Miss Pinkham could do was sigh and say, "Oh dear. I hope the rest of you don't feel that way." If anyone did they didn't answer. Somehow it didn't seem like a question Miss Pinkham wanted an answer to at all.

I tried hard to let Miss Pinkham help me learn and she seemed very pleased whenever I picked something up easily. We hadn't ever gone to school, but Mama had taught us plenty at home. We already knew our letters and numbers, and for some reason the moment those letters were put together it all made perfect sense to me. It was not so easy for Jesse. He threatened to quit almost every day in the beginning. I had to remind him of the real reason we were in school and tell him it didn't matter how much he learned.

"Willie Thompson doesn't care, and there are probably more kids too."

But I knew deep down that Jesse wanted to be learning just as much as me. I knew he longed to pick up a pencil and put down words and have them all make sense. I knew that most of all he didn't want to feel stupid. Willie Thompson wasn't the brightest person around, and whether you said it or not you still thought it. I knew Jesse didn't want to end up like Willie, sleeping his days away with his head resting on his desk. Jesse was too bright for that.

❇ ❇ ❇

The only person who knew Mama's real situation was Reese Buchanan. His was the only help Mama was willing to accept. Reese didn't do a lot of talking. He didn't do a lot of anything without being asked, but when Mama needed a favour he was right there to lend a hand. He took us to town when we needed to go and he helped Jesse with the firewood. When springtime came, he hooked his horse, Ned, up and brought him around to plough us a piece of ground. We didn't have seeds, but he gave us some. He told Mama he had bought too many and that they'd go bad if they weren't put in the ground. I don't think that was the complete truth, but Mama never questioned anything Reese had to say. She tied a rag around her head and sowed every one of the seeds Reese had brought into the ground: beans, peas, lettuce, beets, and cucumbers. As she worked, tiny drops of blood began to drip from her nose, and she asked Jesse to get her a cloth.

"I can finish this, Mama," said Jesse as she sat back on her knees and pressed the cloth to her nose. "Pru and I can do it."

Mama didn't want any part in that. "You've got to learn these things if you're going to make a go of it after I'm gone." She kept dropping the seeds into the dirt one by one and patting the ground down nice and firm. She said for us to watch, to pay close attention. When she was finished she went inside and slept the rest of the day.

Later I saw Davey in the garden, down on his hands and knees. He was pressing his little hand inside Mama's handprints and studying them with the utmost interest. It looked to me like he was trying to commit the pattern to memory, like he knew that quite possibly it would be his last chance at doing so.

I knew Mama had given up waiting to hear anything from Uncle Tom months ago. For weeks and weeks she'd ask if there was a letter for her when Jesse came back from fetching the mail, and each time I'd see that flicker of disappointment in her eyes when Jesse said no.

"Don't you worry about us, Mama," Jesse would say to her, patting her on the back as if she was a small child. "We'll do just fine on our own. I promise. You're teaching us real good."

Chapter Six

The apple blossoms smelled sweet enough to eat that spring. That must have been the way the cedar waxwings felt as I watched them one morning in late May. They were sitting amongst the tree branches, eating all the pretty pink blossoms like hungry, hungry pigs, ripping at the petals and gaping as they struggled to squeeze them down their gullets. What few they left behind blew off the tree the next day and scattered on the ground like big fluffy snowflakes. I picked them up and pressed their silky petals to my lips. It was no wonder that the tree did not manage to produce any apples that year.

It was some time after all the blossoms had gone that a porcupine climbed that very tree early one morning and Jesse shot it. Jesse went to the closet, took Daddy's shotgun out, and with one mighty blast it was over. We all came running, and there was Jesse, holding Daddy's shotgun with a big old grin on his face. Mama brought her hands to her mouth and gasped, not knowing what had just happened. Jesse stepped aside and we saw the porcupine lying in a round ball near his feet. Flora took one look at the porcupine lying dead on the ground and began to cry. She buried her face in Mama's dress and Mama put a gentle hand on her head.

Later, Mama taught Jesse how to skin the porcupine. I cooked it in the oven and we ate it for our supper. Flora cried the whole time it was sizzling in the roaster. We had never eaten porcupine before. We'd never had to.

After that, Mama started thinking. She thought about all the things Gran Hannah had shown her when she was small, all those things that had made her father so angry.

"I'll teach you what you need to know," Mama said to me later. "All the things Gran Hannah showed me. And then I know you'll be fine."

※ ※ ※

Daddy moved us to the deserted farmhouse on the Dalhousie Road sometime after Nanny Gordon passed away. The house belonged to Reese Buchanan, an old-time friend of Daddy's, and Daddy promised to pay Reese a little bit every month to help with the taxes and upkeep.

"If things go right and we get far enough ahead I'll see about buying it one day," Daddy promised.

The only comment Mama made was that the place was surrounded with woods and the woods were filled with enchantment. Mama said she liked trees. Daddy laughed and said, "There's plenty of them here, Issy." And that was no exaggeration.

The house was old, having been built around the turn of the century, nearly eighty years from the time when Lord Dalhousie had marched his men all the way from Annapolis Royal to Halifax. They had blazed a trail through the wilderness as they went, with plans of building a military road through the centre of the province. They'd stopped to rest near the place where the Anglican Church was later built. Some woman by the name of Hutchinson had been in charge of building the church until her husband up and died, and then the frame they had started building blew down in a windstorm one year.

"And the rest got tore down by a bunch of drunken lumbermen," Daddy said, laughing like it was some private joke that only he was in on. Daddy told us these stories about Dalhousie hoping to make it sound like a better place to live and trying to breathe life into this little community, so deep in the wilds of Nova Scotia. The Annapolis Valley was to our north and the South Shore to our south and there we were, smack dab in the middle of it all.

Flora and Davey said they didn't want to move, and Daddy told them they should be right proud to be living in what many would call a "heritage home." Only none of us cared about some lord who trudged through this place over a hundred years before we got here or living in an old rundown house and making it out to be something it wasn't. Why would we care about a church that blew down and got rebuilt? Especially when there were two other churches there and not once had any of us set foot inside a church.

Then one night a few months after we'd moved in, we found Daddy sitting on the steps of that little Anglican Church, singing at the top of his lungs and holding an empty bottle in his hand. It was the happiest I'd seen him in weeks, ever since Elmer Galloway had died and been buried in that very cemetery. Daddy was singing "When Irish Eyes Are Smiling," and when he saw Mama standing there at the foot of the steps he looked down at her and said, "Dammit, woman, you're part Irish. Why aren't you smiling?"

"What have you got there?" Mama asked as she walked up the steps toward Daddy.

"Got? I haven't got a thing," said Daddy, his words coming out slurred and jumbled.

"That's church wine." Mama grabbed the bottle from Daddy and held it up in the moonlight to see.

Davey and Flora giggled and Mama told Jesse and me to take them on home.

"Where did you get that?" I heard Mama ask with annoyance as we walked away, her voice echoing through the clear night air.

"The curtains," he said. "Behind the wine-coloured curtains." Then he started in again, singing a song he'd just made up about drinking on the church steps and making up for all the holy communions he hadn't drank over the years.

Even when we were far down the road, we could still hear Mama chewing Daddy out for getting drunk on the church's wine. Right when I was to the point where I figured we'd all be going to hell someday because of what Daddy did, Jesse began to laugh.

"What's so funny?" I asked, annoyed to think he could find anything remotely amusing about Daddy's disgraceful behavior.

"Just listen."

We stopped in the middle of the road, and there, amidst the peeping of the frogs and the chirping of the crickets, was the long, drawn-out sound of someone's hound dog, baying along to Daddy's rendition of "When Irish Eyes Are Smiling." And then we were all forced to laugh.

Mama went to the church the next morning to talk to the reverend before the service and explain to him as best she could why the parishioners would not be able to have communion. I went with her because it didn't seem right for her to have to go all on her own and confess to something that was all Daddy's doing.

Mama hurried out to the fence as soon as the reverend got out of his car that morning. "I'm afraid Nate drank the communion wine last night," she said.

"I see," said the reverend, giving no indication as to

what he was thinking. His hands were pressed together as through he might be praying and he stood there for a few moments without saying a word. I wondered if he was asking God for patience. I expected that he would be quite angry, but instead he told Mama she should come in for the service. She did as he requested, although I'm sure it was only because of Daddy's deed that she felt obliged to do so.

We sat through the service at the back of the church. When the collection plate came our way, Mama looked at the plate and shook her head apologetically and the man carrying the plate said, "Bless you." Then when the organ started to play and the singing commenced, Mama broke out into song—melodic and sweet, she put the rest of them to shame. I didn't even know Mama knew any hymns, let alone that she could sing them so sweetly.

As we were leaving, the reverend grabbed Mama's hand and held it in his. "You are welcome anytime," he said.

"I trust you'll no longer keep the wine in the church," Mama replied.

Chapter Seven

Reese was a big help right from the very beginning. After we moved into the farmhouse, he mowed the grass with a hand scythe so that Davey and Flora would have a spot to play. We stood back watching as his arms moved in a steady rhythm with each swath he made. Daddy grinned in admiration and told us that Reese was lucky to be alive, let alone out doing work, since he had been stricken with polio at an early age.

"Even that limp of his doesn't slow him down a whole lot," said Daddy. It was easy to see that Daddy was glad to have his old-time friend back in his life.

Reese even built a swing for each of us in the apple trees, though Jesse balked and said he was too old for one.

"You don't need to build me a swing," said Jesse when Reese started to cut out a fourth seat.

"You're never too old to have fun," said Reese.

I knew Jesse was just being stubborn. It wasn't so long ago that he'd play blind man's bluff and hide-and-seek with the rest of us. Ever since we'd moved to Dalhousie he'd been acting moody. One day a few weeks earlier, I'd told Jesse that we didn't like moving all the time any more than he did but he'd just yanked my braid and sent me howling for Mama.

The morning after Reese put up the swings, I saw Jesse cutting through the rope on one of the swings with Mama's paring knife. Daddy threw a fit when he saw what Jesse had done.

"I told Reese I didn't need a swing and I meant it," said Jesse, that stubborn streak of his showing.

I'm not sure who was more stubborn, Daddy or Jesse, because Daddy made Jesse fix the swing even though he complained the whole time.

"Reese put that swing up and that's where it's going to stay," said Daddy matter-of-factly. Mama watched them from the kitchen window, arms folded.

"I sometimes think they're too much alike for their own good," she said, shaking her head with a smile.

※ ※ ※

Reese helped Daddy cut some firewood, and they hauled it out of the woods with Ned. Reese and Daddy split the wood and Jesse and I stacked it up in a pile to dry for the coming winter. All the while they worked at the wood, Daddy grumbled to Reese about Uncle Tom stealing Nanny Gordon's house.

"We'd be living down in Annapolis right now if he'd have gone off to war like the rest of the single men around.

But no, he has to get his trigger finger cut off," Daddy said in a mocking tone. "There's you with that bum leg and me with a family, wanting to stand up for the country if we were able, and then there's people like Tom, making their own excuses."

"Coward!" Jesse's eyes widened. There was contempt in his voice. I knew Jesse fantasized about the war and often played war games with Flora and Davey, but I refused to join in. I thought war was senseless, countries fighting and people killing one another. Wasn't there a better way to settle things? I couldn't imagine there being a good enough reason to be killing people. I didn't even know why someone would want to pretend.

Daddy stood looking at Jesse and me. "Now don't be mentioning to your mother what I told you. She's been making excuses for Tom all her life."

※ ※ ※

Reese and Daddy had to fix things up inside the house too. No one had lived there since Reese's grandfather died and that had been fifteen years or more ago, so there were plenty of things that needed sprucing up. Mama scrubbed the walls and scoured the dirty windows. She sewed curtains to hang and arranged things in the pantry while we ran wild outdoors, playing for hours on end.

"This here's going to be our home from here on out," Daddy said once everything was fixed up. This sounded quite impossible to me, as we were constantly on the move from one house to another, hardly able to make friends at all. Mama just looked at Daddy without saying a word. I think maybe she was thinking the same thing too.

※ ※ ※

Everything went downhill fast after Nanny Gordon died. The funeral was long and tiring. We had to sit at the front of the church and walk past a church full of people on our way up the aisle. We knew Nanny Gordon was lying in that coffin when we walked past even though the lid was down and we could not see her. Outside the church Mama had told us to walk with our heads high and to look straight ahead, not to whisper, and for goodness sake to behave ourselves.

Mama said that funerals bring out the worst in people. I guess she was right, because after Nanny Gordon's funeral we ended up living on the Dalhousie Road in the middle of nowhere and Daddy said it was all Uncle Tom's fault. We were all standing around Nanny Gordon's old house in Annapolis that day. Daddy was smiling and shaking people's hands and I can't remember a time when he seemed happier even though we'd just been to a funeral. Even the minister who had said all those sweet things about Nanny Gordon's good character was there, standing with a small plate and a napkin. People were eating food and sipping tea and saying how nice Nanny Gordon looked wearing her yellow dress and commenting on how the straw bonnet on her head was a nice touch because she was seldom seen outside without that hat. Although their chatter was continual their mood was undoubtedly glum.

The house was crowded with neighbours and cousins when Uncle Tom told Daddy the news he hadn't been expecting to hear: that he would be staying in Nanny's big old house and that it had all been set down on paper. Daddy was furious with both Uncle Tom and Nanny Gordon. Although I'm not sure if it's proper to hold a grudge against someone who just died, I do know it's not at all proper to air your dirty laundry in public.

"You don't even have a family," said Daddy. "It's just you. You to live in this big house all by yourself. I can't believe you tricked the old lady into this." A hush fell over the entire household. You could have heard a pin drop.

"Tom did help look after Nanny these last months," Mama said in a half-hearted attempt at diplomacy. She could see that Daddy was about to burst out in anger. We all could.

"Did you want to move down here and live with your mother? You with four young ones to contend with?" Daddy asked her with a vile stare. I could feel a whole room full of eyes set upon us, throwing out daggers of surprise, shock, and utter loathing. Everyone in Annapolis loved Nanny Gordon.

"Well, no," Mama stumbled. "But it's not like you think. I had my hands full," she added looking around at the crowd of people who stood waiting for some explanation, as if it had just dawned on them and they were all thinking, *That's right! Why weren't you looking after your mother?*

"And you shouldn't have had to," continued Daddy. "This was promised to you years ago, Issy. Years ago. No strings attached."

"It wasn't really promised, Nate." Daddy's face turned bright red as if he was embarrassed that Mama did not agree with him.

"The insinuation was there.... Look at him!" said Daddy, pointing toward Uncle Tom. "Who has he got? No one. Just himself. He doesn't need a house."

Uncle Tom cleared his throat and gave Mama an apologetic look. "Dad signed the place over years ago. Mum had no say. Her name was never on the deed," he said to Mama. "I thought you knew."

"It's not your fault," whispered Mama, touching Uncle Tom's arm right before Daddy grabbed hold of her other arm and hauled her out the front door.

"Come on," Daddy said to all of us as we stood there dazed at the scene that had just taken place in Nanny Gordon's beautiful old house. Daddy had always said that the house would be ours one day even though we had never quite understood that Nanny Gordon would no longer be alive when at last we came there to live.

I'm not sure who was more upset about us not getting Nanny Gordon's house, Daddy or Jesse. As soon as we were outside, Jesse turned back toward the house, shouting horrible things and calling Uncle Tom all sorts of ugly names. When he picked up a rock and got ready to throw it, Mama ran toward Jesse and grabbed hold of his arm.

"Come on, Jesse," she cried as she pulled on him. Jesse wrenched away quickly, angry that Mama had stopped him, and marched past all of us.

※ ※ ※

I sometimes wondered if Daddy would have gone to Ontario to pick tobacco that summer if Mama had been sick. He said he was tired of working in the woods. That's all there was to do in Dalhousie, and he wasn't all that sure his back would hold up. But there was another reason why Daddy didn't want to work in the woods and it had nothing to do with how lame his back was. In May of that year, while Daddy was clear-cutting on company land, a tree landed on Elmer Galloway, flattening him into the ground. Daddy was there when Elmer took his last breath, gasping like a fish out of water. Deaf old Elmer didn't hear Daddy when he called out "Timber!" So even though Daddy didn't say it, I knew that was the reason he didn't want to work in the woods anymore and even the reason he stole the communion wine and sang on the church steps a few weeks after Elmer was buried in the churchyard. I knew and I'm sure Mama knew.

Daddy said we'd be fine while he was gone because he was leaving Jesse behind to look after us all, and Jesse looked real proud to be left in charge. Daddy said he would send us money as soon as he was paid, and that there was nothing for any of us to worry about.

"I'll be home once the harvest is over," he promised.

Chapter Eight

The June wind tugged at the clothes in Pru's hands as she struggled to pin them fast to the clothesline. Flora stood by to hand her each piece, jabbering away about a cluster of monarch butterflies that were sipping nectar from the lilac bush growing next to the house. Flora said she liked the way their wings opened and closed and asked Pru if she thought that Mama was one of those butterflies, come back to see them.

"Mama's not a butterfly," Pru told her.

"How do you know she isn't?" Flora asked, reaching into the wash basket for another article of clothing.

"Because if Mama was anything she'd be an eagle, not a fragile thing like a butterfly that lives for one day and then dies dead in the dirt," said Pru. Flora did not say anything more about the butterflies.

Pru thought afterward that it was mean of her to say what she did just to keep her sister quiet. Sometimes Flora's jabbering exasperated Pru to the point where she was ready to throw her hands up in the air, especially when she had other things on her mind, such as now.

※ ※ ※

One of the things Mama had told Pru before she died was that folks sometimes see little things that aren't right—they notice the smoke coming from your chimney and whether the curtains have been moved. She'd told Pru that they needed to be careful so as not to cause suspicion.

Not long after Mama died, Pru started hanging her mother's clothes out on the line for the neighbours to see. Mama had adored seeing the clothes dangling on the clothesline—reds and blues and greens, a whole mish-mash of colours parading about in the wind. Most of all she'd adored seeing the white sheets billowing out like parachutes in a puff of air, flapping and fluttering with ease. There was only one set of white sheets that had not been patched in at least three or four places. Uncle Tom had sent them to Mama brand new along with a whole parcel of things that had belonged to Nanny Gordon.

"I thought it was only fair that you have some of Mum's things," Uncle Tom had written in his note.

"Crumbs!" Daddy had said as he rummaged through the items Uncle Tom had sent. Reaching into the box, he picked up one of the items and said, "Look at that, an old yellowed doily. It's not even new," and threw it carelessly back into the box.

"Mum made that with her own hands. It's a keepsake, for sentimental reasons," Mama had said, removing it from the box and stretching it out in her fingers.

"Look at you. He sends you crumbs and thinks every-thing's going to be all right," Daddy had said, standing in front of Mama all red-faced with anger.

"He didn't have to send anything, Nate. He didn't have to send a thing."

"You do it back up and return it," Daddy had said.

"I can't do that. What will he think?" Mama had pro-tested. They'd argued back and forth for a time until finally, through a veil of tears, Mama had given in.

"Either you do it or I will," Daddy had said finally. "And when you're done, you just write a note and tell him what he can do with his crumbs," he'd added, which Mama had out and out refused to do. So Daddy had written the note him-self. He'd carried the parcel off to the Dale post office that day while Mama had watched from the doorway crying.

The day Daddy left to pick tobacco in Ontario, Mama had removed the sheets from the package and put them on her bed. If Daddy had known she'd kept those sheets, he would have hit the roof. Mama had smiled as she tucked them under the mattress. "I've never slept on brand-spanking-new sheets before," she'd said.

But after Mama had gotten sick she'd told Pru to take them up for fear that she would suffer a nosebleed through the night and the stains would set before morning. She'd said she couldn't bear to see them hanging dingy on the clothesline.

※ ※ ※

With Flora still chattering, Pru did not hear Mrs. McFarland come up behind her as she dragged the clothes basket along, pinning the clothes fast to the line.

"Pru…Pru Burbidge!"

Pru let out a loud gasp and turned. Flora dropped Mama's pretty flowered dress in the grass.

"A beautiful day to be hanging out a wash," said Mrs. McFarland. "Isadora is lucky to have such help."

Pru couldn't think of an earthly word to say. She had not seen Mrs. McFarland since the day she had stormed from the house. Mrs. McFarland meant trouble in one form or another—that was why Mama had sent her away—and Pru knew she had to keep Mrs. McFarland from nosing around.

"I haven't seen Isadora in ages. Used to be I'd see her at Hurley's store from time to time," said Mrs. McFarland, eyeing Pru with a look of displeasure.

Pru looked at Flora and Flora looked at Pru. "Mama says Hurley's is a poor excuse for a store. She's been doing her shopping in town."

"Oh she does, does she?" said Mrs. McFarland with a great deal of indignation, which indicated that she was not at all pleased with what Pru had just told her. And it was no wonder, as Pru remembered just then that Emily McFarland and Mrs. Hurley were related to each other in some way. "The Hurleys have served this community very well over the years, but I suppose newcomers might not appreciate it."

"They're handy enough for some things," said Pru in an attempt to smooth things over. "Mama says at least it's not far to go in a pinch."

"And I'd suspect your mother has had reason to accept their generosity from time to time." Mrs. McFarland was being smug about the fact that Mama, like other people in the community, had received markdowns at the store from time to time. The Hurleys were not as discreet as they should be about divulging such information.

It was then that Mrs. McFarland looked at the clothing that Pru and Flora were hanging on the line. Mama's dresses mixed in with the wet laundry, dry as snuff.

"Why, these don't even look like they've been washed!" she exclaimed.

Pru thought playing dumb might be to her advantage, so she did not offer up any explanation. Mrs. McFarland grabbed hold of one of Mama's dresses from the line and turned back toward Pru, looking like Ned did when he flapped his lips while trying to pick a blade of grass up from an open palm.

"Why, Pru Burbidge, I have no doubt that you know exactly what you are doing, although for the life of me I can't figure out why. You're as odd as the day is long," said Mrs. McFarland. "No one puts out perfectly dry clothes.

Surely you've got more to do with your time. What does your mother have to say about all this, you out here hanging her good dresses on the line? Are you girls playing?"

"Playing? I…I…Mama asked me to," Pru said.

"Well, that's just ridiculous. No one in their right mind would ask you to do such a thing. I must ask your mother what's wrong with her head." Mrs. McFarland began trotting toward the house.

Pru knew she had to say something to stop Mrs. McFarland. "They needed airing!" she cried out. Mrs. McFarland spun around on her heels. "The clothes cupboard was damp. Mama said her dresses needed airing."

"Airing?" She sounded doubtful. "It's a bit late in the year for airing, wouldn't you say?" Pru held her breath, hoping Mrs. McFarland would drop her line of questioning. "Of course, no one pays attention to any of the old ways any more. Why, Rachel Lamb doesn't even air her bedding any more. She goes from one season to the next without giving it a second thought. Not so long ago they dragged everything out of the house in April and scrubbed the house from top to bottom."

"Mama says it's a shame that folks don't air their laundry more often and it's positively scandalous that the cleaning ritual she grew up knowing has gone to the crows." Pru bit her lip, wishing she hadn't rambled on so. Mrs. McFarland gave Pru the most peculiar look.

"I may as well drop in to see Isadora while I'm here. I know we ended things on a sour note the last time around, but we're neighbours nonetheless. I always liked your mother, Pru. And I'll admit to feeling guilty over my last departure," she said with as much righteousness as she could muster. "It can't be easy for Isadora, what with your father up and leaving. I'm sure she would appreciate a visit."

Pru could sense her hesitancy, as if she was waiting to be told that it was indeed a good idea for her to go in uninvited.

"You can't do that," said Pru point-blank. By this time Flora was hightailing it toward the house, pigtails bouncing behind her.

"Can't?" Mrs. McFarland squeaked.

"It's just that Mama's not home," Pru said.

"Not home?"

"She's gathering things," Pru said, realizing that likely sounded utterly silly to someone like Mrs. McFarland.

But Mama's place more rightly seemed in the woods, with all the time she used to spend exploring the wooded area behind the house. "I belong in the woods," she used to say. Gran Hannah used to take Mama to the woods when she was small, telling her about the things that grew there, which plants could heal and which ones might kill you stone dead.

But after Gran Hannah had died, Mama's father had

told her she should forget all that foolishness. "Your grandmother was an Indian, but you aren't. You're Irish like your mother," he'd told her.

"You are a strange one, Pru Burbidge," declared Mrs. McFarland, with her nose stuck up in the air.

Pru smiled and said she didn't know what that meant and then Mrs. McFarland let a most unladylike noise escape from her mouth and marched away.

Chapter Nine

Sweet fern. Teaberries. Juniper. Black spruce.

Sometimes morning leaps into my bedroom window and I wake from a deep sleep trying to remember what all those plants are for, what medicines Gran Hannah used to make even though Mama's father did not want her to. Mama and Gran Hannah hid what they were doing because they were forced to, not because they wanted to.

"And it was a shame," Mama said. "Gran Hannah made a poultice for Tom after the cow kicked him and my father became so angry. Before that day I didn't even know how he felt."

I often close my eyes and picture myself in the middle of the forest or by the edge of the stream or next to the meadow, all the places Mama used to take us. Sometimes I can almost hear the gurgling water skimming the moss-covered rocks in the creek. I imagine all the berries and the leaves Mama showed me. Every one of them had a special name, a special purpose.

Green was everywhere, so strong and pungent that the air was packed full with the aroma of ferns and leaves.

The sun fell through the treetops, leaving patches of light and shadow on the forest floor, and we played a kind of hopscotch with the sun, jumping from one spot to the next. Every once in a while Mama would call out to us to slow down.

Witch hazel. Bayberry. Willow bark.

Mama told me and told me so many times, and I wish now that I'd written everything down instead of trying to keep it all in my head. Gran Hannah knew what these plants were used for and she left the names behind for Mama. Mama said she'd forgotten plenty over the years but the more time she spent walking in the woods the more it began to come back to her.

"I promised Gran Hannah I wouldn't let these things be forgotten," Mama said. "My father was ashamed of who he was and he thought he could make a better life for us. He didn't want people to know."

Gold thread.

"You'll find it in the earth," Mama said. "As thin and bright as thread made of spun gold. It is a perfect name." Tearing the mossy soil away, she dug into the ground until she found what she was looking for. "It might help with my appetite," she said, and I thought about how nice it would be to have Mama sit at the table and eat a hearty meal, although I doubted it was at all possible, even with the gold thread tonic.

"Gran Hannah used to steep it right in the kitchen when my father was gone." She gave a small laugh. "There was no stopping that one, no matter what my father said. I tried a sip once and it was bitter as old heck, but Mum would drink it down without batting an eye. It's a wonder her stomach didn't bother her more often, as hard as my father was," she added.

One day in late August Mama asked me to go for a walk in the woods with her. "Just Pru. This time is for Pru and I," she said when Flora and Davey whined that they wanted to go too.

Mama was weak but did not complain. From time to time, she held fast to my arm for support. Although Mama did not tell me her reasons for wanting to go for a hike so deep in the woods that day, it seemed to me that as weak as she was and as many times as we stopped to rest, she moved with a certainty in her steps, her head held high with conviction. We walked until we were standing on top of an overhang looking down into a small ravine.

"I found this place by accident right after we moved here," said Mama. I stood looking at Mama, at her arms stretched upward toward the sky, as a yellow ray of sunlight broke through the clouds and touched her skin. Her face transformed, the lines and shadows disappeared. It was as if she'd been made well by some secret cure. I wanted to laugh out loud and clap my hands, but then the sun slipped back into the cloud and I could see that nothing had changed.

"It's the perfect place, Pru. No worries or cares, just the wind and the trees and the earth beneath your feet. If I could keep this moment forever, I would," she said, and took my hand in hers.

A light breeze fell across my face, like an invisible hand caressing me with long, even strokes. Mama's hair trailed out behind her and the fabric of her dress flapped each time the wind picked up a bit. Far off in the distance a tree stood out in the open. A handful of its orange leaves waved at us across the gap and I told Mama I had never seen such a strange sight as autumn leaves in the summertime.

"The world is filled with many strange things, so many that you couldn't count them all even if you wanted to. But it's not the knowing of everything there is in the world so much as it is the imagining of all there could be," she said. I wasn't sure I knew what she meant, but her words seemed to bring me comfort.

For the longest while we stood on top of the bluff, listening to the birds and the wind and the deep rumbling sounds of bullfrogs echoing up from a nearby marsh, spellbound by the sights and sounds of nature all around us.

"Can you feel Gran Hannah, Pru? Her strength, her wisdom?" asked Mama.

I wasn't altogether sure I could, but I said yes anyway.

"Sometimes I hear her voice in the wind. I look around but she's never there. She seems so close. I've seen her in my dreams, Pru. I know it sounds silly, but I've felt her touch upon my skin." Mama looked over at me and smiled, hooking a strand of hair behind my ear. "You're so much like her. I've known it for a while now. You lead with your heart but you use your head too. That's what strength is, Pru, holding it all in even when you're aching to let it out. You are a wise girl."

"No I'm not, Mama." I knew I was anything but wise. How could Mama say such a thing and mean it?

Mama smiled and told me that one day I would understand what she was talking about.

"There are all kinds of wisdom in the world, Pru. It's in everything from a sunrise to a dewdrop. It doesn't have to be complicated. Complicating things is our own doing. We're handed life on a platter. It should be so easy," said Mama as she clasped her hand around the delicate golden thread she had dug from the earth. There was sadness in her voice.

Sometimes I go to the woods by myself just to listen to the birds and the squirrels and the sound of the trees. I hold my face toward the sky and let the wind touch my cheeks. I breathe in the colours, the sights, sounds, and smells. I think of the old people, the first ones in this country, even though Mama always said you'd have to stretch us out mighty thin to find that drop of Indian blood in us. I try to imagine I'm one of them, wise in the ways that will one day count.

Then I go home.

❊ ❊ ❊

One evening Mama showed me the metal tin in her dresser drawer and made me count the money that was inside. My hand trembled when I reached in and removed the paper bills. There was more money in that little tin than I had ever thought of seeing at one time. Through all her years of penny-pinching and making do, Mama had put a small fortune aside: a whole big stack of ones, twos, and five dollar bills—money not even Daddy knew she had. She admitted that she had started saving before we moved to Dalhousie.

"Your uncle Tom slipped me a hundred dollars after the funeral," she said. "Shoved it in my dress pocket with your father standing right there in the room. He said that Mum wanted me to have it. And it was fair of him, Pru. He didn't have to do it. I've thought about it at least a hundred times, the fact that he didn't have to give me anything. But I couldn't tell your father. You know what you father was like. When he had his mind made up about something there was no one could change it. I knew if I told him it would just set him off again. Look how he behaved when Tom sent that parcel. And the honest truth was I didn't know what he'd do with the money. I thought he'd waste it on something we didn't need. Your father was impulsive that way. A man with big dreams."

I could hear the desperation in her voice as she tried to explain it all to me. When she was finished talking, she took my hand in hers. "Tom isn't a bad man, Pru, no matter what your father thought," she said with a sigh. I guess him giving that money to Mama proved it, at least in her mind.

"This money will keep the family together after I'm gone," she told me. "It's for you and Jesse to know about and no one else."

"Don't worry, Mama. I promise we won't waste it."

"Now it won't hurt to buy a treat now and then. Remember the peppermint candies we bought right after the first baby bonus cheque came?"

I nodded. How could I possibly forget, as happy as Mama had been that day?

"But you shouldn't make a habit of it. There are many things out there that will tempt you, but your brothers and sister must come first."

I made all the promises Mama asked me to make before she closed the tin.

"If you ever need to leave, you go straight to Reese Buchanan. He'll help you. This money will take you wherever you need to go." There was a look of satisfaction on Mama's face.

"I promise, Mama. We'll go to Reese if we need to."

And that was the very last promise I made to Mama.

Then I asked Mama how we would ever manage without her and Mama's answer came without hesitation.

"You might not see me but I'll still be around," she said, "like the breeze that comes from out of nowhere on a hot summer day. And when you find yourself smiling for no reason in the world, a part of me will be smiling too."

"I won't smile once you're gone," I said.

"It may take a while, Pru, but your smile will come back. That's why we have to celebrate all the little things we do, because some day you'll look back and remember what that smile felt like," said Mama. I knew Mama was wrong, my smile would never return. How could it? It had slipped from the face of the earth like the setting sun, and it would never rise again.

"We all have our time, Pru. And we don't get to choose how long it will last. My time's not up yet," Mama whispered. "Not yet."

I buried my face into Mama's pillow and she touched my head gently.

"I hope you understand why I kept some things from your father," she added. "Not all secrets are bad, Pru. Sometimes it's better to keep the peace than to lay everything out on the table."

I could not look Mama in the eye when she said that. A

queer feeling snaked through me, a feeling so strange that it caused my heart to flutter. I thought suddenly about what Jesse had done and the secret I had kept from Mama all these months. I should have spoken up right then and there; it was my chance and I let it slip away. But I couldn't bear to see the disappointment in her eyes. A deed done and over is a deed that cannot be taken back. So how could I have possibly told Mama the truth that night?

※ ※ ※

At the time, Jesse said it was for the best. He said that Uncle Tom was a thief and Mama was far too trusting. He held the letter up toward the sky and tried to look through the envelope.

"Maybe you should have just asked Mama what she wrote." Jesse's curiosity annoyed me.

"It really doesn't matter what she wrote," said Jesse. "Uncle Tom's never going to read it."

"No, Jesse!" I cried out, running toward him. But it was too late. I watched in horror as Jesse tore the letter to shreds and burned the pieces in the middle of the road.

"Mama would trust a thief if she caught him with his hand in the cookie jar," Jesse said as the fire finally died out.

"Jesse, you shouldn't have! What will Mama say?" I knew this was wrong. So very wrong.

"Mama's not going to know if you don't tell her. Look,

Pru, Mama thinks Uncle Tom can do no wrong. But it doesn't change what he did. You know what that house meant to Daddy, to all of us. Mama thinks because he's her brother that it doesn't matter what he did. But it does matter. We both know Daddy never would have left if we'd been living in that house down in Annapolis."

I thought about Jesse's words and I could see some truth in what he said. For many years, all Daddy had ever talked about was that house of Nanny Gordon's. I know he tried to be happy in Dalhousie and sometimes he'd even had me convinced that he was, but that all changed after Elmer Galloway died. Everything about Daddy seemed to change after that.

"We'll be fine," Jesse said. "You and I are doing it all now anyway, and we've got Reese."

I knew Jesse was right; we were doing it all. We had both grown so much over the past year, and perhaps I should be ashamed to say it, but it was far easier to trust in Jesse's words than to put trust in Uncle Tom, who I hardly even knew. And so, right or wrong, I kept Jesse's secret, hoping I wouldn't regret it later. If we had only known then how sick Mama really was it might have made a big difference.

※ ※ ※

Flora and I sleep in Mama's bed now, on the white sheets Uncle Tom sent her. When it is cold or windy, or simply if she's scared, Flora curls into a tight ball beside me. Some nights I sing to her, but mostly we talk about all the celebrations and the happy times we had with Mama. We talk about the pink slippers that Reese Buchanan helped us buy at the rummage sale and those nights when Mama would call us to her room so we could watch for the first evening star. Mama always said the first star would grant us our wishes, and even if it didn't it was always fun to pretend. After we wished on the first star, we would play the "If only…" game, shouting out things like "If only I had a mink coat" or "If only I had a grand piano." For the longest time, Flora's "If only…" always ended with "If only Daddy would come home."

Now, as we lie next to each other in Mama's bed, Flora and I talk about all the happy times, savouring them like peppermint candies in our mouths, and then we go to sleep.

Deadly nightshade.

Sometimes before I drift off to sleep I think those words and it makes me angry. But then I think how selfish it is of me to be angry with Mama. There is a truth about the deadly nightshade, a truth only Mama knows. So I forget my anger and whisper softly to Mama, hoping that one day she will tell me that truth.

Chapter Ten

The very next day after Mrs. McFarland nearly barged into the house, Daddy came home. He arrived on the back of someone's truck with an old brown bag slung over his shoulder, wearing a tweed cap that covered his eyes. There were days and perhaps months when I would have welcomed the sight of him without a bit of hesitancy, but now that he was within my sight I had to resist the urge to run away and hide. Strings of emotion were twining through me and I wasn't sure which ones to trust. I watched as Daddy's stride hastened with each step he made until he all but burst through the front door. I stood still for only a few moments and the instant he smiled at me I ran toward his open arms. I couldn't help myself.

Daddy was home at long last! Everything would be better. All our worries could be thrown out the window and forgotten. There was so much to tell him that I had no idea where to begin, and a flood of words threatened to burst from my lips. I wanted to sob and laugh and shout alleluia all at the same time. But I knew I couldn't allow it.

I had aged too much over the past year to let some child-
ish outburst betray me. I had learned to be strong just like
Gran Hannah, and was not about to forget Mama's les-
sons just because Daddy was back. The amount of times I
had explained things out to him when he wasn't there to
hear I couldn't begin to count. Now here he was. He was
here to hear it all, to listen and understand. I would begin
with Mama of course. That was the most important part.
I'd start with Mama and the rest would follow.

But before I had time to explain anything Davey and
Flora came through the doorway. The moment they saw
Daddy they rushed to him in a wild flurry, both vying for
the same place in Daddy's open arms. Daddy cradled them
both at once, smothering them in a barrage of kisses.

Jesse did not look so happy. He kept a safe distance,
as if he had something to fear, or else was bitten with
resentment, as he watched Flora and Davey clamour for
Daddy's affection. I could tell by the look on Jesse's face
that it angered him to see the way they cooed and went on
about Daddy's being there.

Later, as we stood beside the spot where Mama was
buried, our heads bowed, all holding hands because
Daddy said it seemed only decent to do so, a soft wind
whistled through the treetops and I knew it was Mama
looking down at us from above. Daddy picked a bouquet
of buttercups and daisies to place at the top of Mama's

grave and told us we should always remember to pick Mama fresh flowers.

"You know how much Issy loved flowers," he said.

But Flora protested, explaining that Mama had told us not to put any flowers on her grave because people might see them and wonder.

"It won't matter now what people see," said Daddy.

⁂ ⁂ ⁂

Finally Daddy asked me to tell him about the sickness that took Mama away. As hard as it was, I told him all that I could remember—all but the very last part, as it was too upsetting. Only it had been bothering me, you see: the tea that Mama drank that night, the tea I had prepared for Mama, and then Mama dying like that through the night. Some days it troubled me more than others. But I could not voice my fears to anyone. What if I was wrong? What if there was nothing sinister about the tea Mama drank right before she died?

When I was finished the story, I wondered if maybe Daddy could tell there were missing parts, but if he did he didn't mention it. He listened quietly to what I had to say, giving me his full attention. I spoke slowly and steadily, aware of a gentle rhythm to my voice, as I named out all the things we had celebrated over the course of Mama's illness. "Mama said we'd remember things better that way," I told him.

I told Daddy what a good friend Reese Buchanan had been to us, and how Mama had said Reese would help with the burying only Jesse said it was something we needed to do all on our own.

"You've become quite independent," said Daddy, smiling tenderly at Jesse. "Issy taught you well."

"It's too late now, with Mama dead and buried," Jesse said fiercely. "Where were you when she was sick and we needed your help?" Jumping up from the table, he pushed his chair aside. It fell to the floor as he hurried out the front door.

I looked at Daddy, sorry that he had to see this, and followed Jesse outside.

"I can't pretend everything's fine," Jesse said, looking out toward the Dalhousie Road. "Daddy brought us out here to the middle of nowhere and took off. He didn't care what happened. For a long time I thought he'd come back, but I was a stupid kid who didn't know any better."

"Things aren't always the way they seem to be on the outside," I said to Jesse, sharing in his disappointment at Daddy's behaviour. I knew Jesse was right—Daddy owed us some sort of explanation. But a part of me couldn't help but wish these past two years away, pretend like they had never happened. How much easier it would be.

I tried to use words that I thought Mama might say. Mama, who was forgiving and generous by nature, who never once badmouthed Daddy to any of us after he left.

Even if Jesse thought it was too late, I knew otherwise.

"It's still Daddy, Jesse. Right or wrong, that part hasn't changed. We should hear what he has to say, at least for Flora and Davey's sake. All they know is that Daddy's back. Don't you remember all those nights Flora cried?"

Jesse spun around to face me. "Who took Daddy's place these past two years? Who chopped wood and snared rabbits and kept Davey and Flora safe? Who made sure we had food on the table and kept fires going in the winter when it was so cold the windows froze up during the night? Who went to school all at the same time so that the government money would keep coming?"

"And you did everything the way Mama asked, Jesse, things we couldn't have done without you," I replied. "But you don't have to do it all now. You can just be yourself like everyone else. Go swimming in the brook or sit out under a tree just like before. You don't have to take Daddy's place anymore."

"But what if he takes off again, Pru? What will we do then? He did it once; what makes you so sure he won't do it again?" The intensity had disappeared from his voice. I could tell that my words were beginning to break him down.

"Because Mama's gone now, Jesse. Everything's changed."

His eyes softened at the mention of Mama's name. He

did not say anything for a long while.

"Okay, I'll come back inside," he finally said. "But I'll do it for you and Mama, Pru. Not for him."

※ ※ ※

I sliced bread for our supper and opened two of the jars of applesauce that I'd canned last fall from the wild apples Davey and Jesse had found one day in September. I steeped tea and poured a cup for Daddy and hoped he would be pleased that I'd learned to make bread and put down food while he'd been gone. But most of all I hoped he'd be pleased with the wood Jesse had chopped and stacked up so nice and high.

Later in the evening, Daddy told us about Ontario and the big tobacco field where he'd worked and how it was back-breaking work but still better than chopping wood. He told us that it was so hot there that the sun could dry up a raindrop the second it touched the ground. He spoke about the huge rain barrel heated by the sun that the tobacco pickers showered beneath every evening before supper. He talked long into the evening.

"But now it's time for you two to go to bed," he said, smiling at Flora and Davey.

"Not yet! Not yet!" they cried as Jesse and I took them off to their beds.

As the evening wore on, the sky darkened and the rain started. Daddy said the rain would be good for the beans we had planted and he asked if we had planted last spring too. Jesse spoke up and said that Mama had planted everything by herself, even though the blackflies had her chewed to pieces, and that she hadn't stopped, not even after she got a nosebleed.

"We'll pickle down some beans this year, and some cucumbers," said Daddy, ignoring Jesse's outburst.

"We did that last fall, even though Mama was too sick and weak to help," put in Jesse.

There was a long silence before Daddy said anything. "I know you're angry, Jesse, and I don't much blame you. All I can say is that I'm here now."

"A few words can't fix this for you. You had no business going in the first place," said Jesse defiantly, folding his arms in front of him.

"I went for the work. It was to be a few months while the harvest was on. I sent money home. But then things went wrong." There was regret in Daddy's voice. I could hear it. And I wished Jesse would stop picking apart everything Daddy had to say and just listen for a moment.

"Everyone from here was going, Jesse. Pete Norwood, Martin Hirtle, Jake Adams."

"And don't forget Nate Burbidge," added Jesse spitefully. "Only you know what? He's the only one who never came back. The rest of them did. They looked after their families. Who did you look after, Daddy? Yourself, that's who."

I thought about the day Jake Adams had come to the house with the money that was owed to Daddy, money he said that Daddy had never bothered to come back to collect.

"I figured you could use it," said Jake. Mama thanked him, but I knew she was embarrassed when she took the envelope of money from Jake. Jake said no one was sure what had happened to Daddy. "One day he just didn't show up for work."

Daddy sat at the table with his head down. I wanted to tell Jesse that he should be ashamed of himself, but I couldn't bring myself to utter the words. A part of me understood his disappointment and anger because I had felt those same things too. I wanted to trust Daddy and yet something niggled at me, a faint whisper off in the background warning me to be cautious, not to trust too quickly.

"I ran into a little trouble in Ontario," Daddy finally admitted.

"What kind of trouble?" I asked, instantly fearing the answer.

"You don't need to hear the details. Let's just say I was in the wrong place at the wrong time. When you're a nobody no one will give you a listen. Didn't even get to tell my side of things," said Daddy with slight indignation.

"You were in jail?" I wasn't prepared for the surprised tone in Jesse's voice when he asked the question. I could tell he was as shocked as I was. Daddy didn't say much after that. He just sat by the window and looked out at the rain.

❋ ❋ ❋

The very next day Daddy mentioned that the food situation was a bit poor, not to mention the fact that we hadn't planned on an extra mouth to feed. I brought ten dollars out from the tin box in Mama's dresser drawer and asked him to pick up some groceries at Hurley's.

Later, Jesse told me he couldn't believe what I'd done.

"You just watch. He'll take that money and go off on a drunk."

"Then that's something we need to know," I said. "It should be worth ten dollars to know that much. Shouldn't it?"

Jesse waited out on the doorstep for Daddy to come home. Twice he came inside, impatient over the fact that Daddy hadn't yet returned.

"Hurley's isn't that far away," he said. I knew he was wondering if Daddy was drinking up the money and if he would come crawling back a few days later asking for forgiveness the way he used to with Mama.

When Reese's car pulled up with Daddy sitting in the front seat, we ran out to see what he had brought.

"Reese was on his way to New Germany this morning, so I figured who needs Hurley's?" said Daddy, smiling as he climbed out of Reese's car. He reached into the grocery

box and pulled out some licorice candy for Flora and
Davey. Jesse took the box from Daddy and examined its
contents as he headed toward the house.

❋ ❋ ❋

Toward nightfall, as I was walking past the kitchen window,
I noticed Daddy sitting on one of the swings Reese made
for us when we first arrived in Dalhousie. He looked so
forlorn sitting out there by himself, looking in the direction of Mama's grave. I quietly slipped out the back door,
resisting the urge to call out his name. He appeared to be
deep in thought. He didn't hear me approach, and didn't
look up until I took my place on the swing beside him.

"You should come in, Daddy," I said. "It's getting dark.
Flora and Davy will want you to tuck them in." For a time
the only sounds to be heard were the chorus of frogs and
Jesse's muffled voice from inside the house ushering the
younger ones off to bed.

"You and Jesse are doing a great job here. You don't
need me at all, do you?" he asked. There was a melancholy
tone in his voice that blended with the soft night sounds
around us.

"Of course we need you! We'll always need you," I said.

"You don't need your mother. People die and life goes
on and if I died tomorrow you'd still be fine. You and Jesse
are just about grown. Jesse'll soon be holding down a job.
Do you know how old I was when I started working?"

I nodded. I knew the story well, how Daddy went off to work when he was thirteen because there wasn't anyone left to look after him.

Daddy held a small bottle to his lips. There was no mistaking the smell of vanilla extract. I knew I wouldn't dare tell Jesse that Daddy was drinking, that he'd bought vanilla extract with some of the money I had given him.

"I'm a poor excuse for a man, Pru. I've made my share of mistakes," he said, screwing the top back on the bottle. "And I'll make more before all is said and done."

"Mama used to say that there are no mistakes, just hurdles we need to get over," I said, hoping that Mama's words would strike a note in him.

"Issy." There was a smile in his voice when he mentioned Mama's name.

I placed my hand on his elbow as we got up off the swings and headed toward the house.

※ ※ ※

Two days later Daddy was gone, along with his bag and shoes and coat. Gone without a trace. All day long we waited for his return. When twilight settled among the trees and the birds fell silent for the night I went to Mama's dresser drawer and took out the tin box. The money was gone. I didn't need to wonder where it went.

Chapter Eleven

The first to come was Mr. Dixon.

Pru was in the garden, kneeling and pulling out the weeds around the cucumber plants. Jesse was busy hoeing the beans. Davey was pushing Flora on the swing, laughing as Flora kicked her legs each time she went up in the air.

Mr. Dixon parked his car beside the road and slammed the door shut. He marched toward the house like a man on a mission, his arms swinging at his side. Jesse put down his hoe and went to head Mr. Dixon off, but instead Mr. Dixon walked right past Jesse and into the house, calling out Mama's name as he went from one room to another. Pru, Davey, and Flora all ran for the house.

"What are you doing?" Jesse cried, but Mr. Dixon didn't stop.

"Leave us alone," Pru called out as she hurried to keep up to Mr. Dixon, who by this time was opening doors and closets like the place belonged to him. He climbed the stairs and searched in each of the bedrooms.

"I'll leave you alone as soon as I talk to Isadora. Now where is she?" he asked, turning to go back down the stairs.

"She's not here," said Jesse.

Pru's heart pummelled like the wings of a humming bird. Had her deepest fears come to pass? Would they be found out and sent to live in foster homes, the family torn apart the way Mama had feared? This just couldn't be happening.

"Where is she? I've been told that she's not alive, that she passed on some time ago. Is that the truth, son? I hope for all your sakes that it isn't."

"No sir, it's not. It's not the least bit true," said Jesse, looking Mr. Dixon straight in the eye.

"You wouldn't be lying to me, would you? How old are you?"

"Fourteen," answered Jesse. Pru thought she could detect a trace of fear in her brother's voice.

"Fourteen? The law might go easy on you," said Mr. Dixon, looking at Jesse with stern determination, as if he was set on getting to the bottom of this.

Thumping down the steps, Mr. Dixon headed for the back door. All four Burbidges trailed behind. They looked at one another, juggling a ball of fear back and forth like a hot potato. Was everything they had struggled for about to tumble to the ground?

"I was told there's a grave out here somewhere," said Mr. Dixon, shaking his head.

Pru's eyes rested on the wildflowers they had placed on

Mama's grave two days earlier when Daddy was home. Luckily the flowers had wilted into the grass, decomposed past the point of recognition.

"It had better not be true, or you'll have a lot to answer for." Before Mr. Dixon could take another step, Jesse ran to face him. Jesse grabbed Mr. Dixon by the shoulder and pushed him backwards.

"This is our home, Mr. Dixon, and Mama's not going to be very pleased when she comes back. Then we'll see who's in trouble with the law," he said.

Mr. Dixon relaxed his shoulders, let out a sigh, and pulled his hands through his hair. "I might have jumped the gun," he said. "But I got a call. And Isadora hasn't been seen in months.... People are talking..." His voice trailed away to empty air.

"Leave or it may be your last time to leave," Jesse said, seeing that he now had the upper hand. Davey and Flora gave Pru a bewildered look. Had Jesse just threatened to harm Mr. Dixon? It sounded that way to Pru. This was not good. Not good at all.

The moment Mr. Dixon left, Pru sunk slowly to the floor and buried her hands in her face. This was all going terribly wrong. It wasn't supposed to be this way. Not this way at all.

"How did he know?" Jesse demanded as he watched out the window to make sure Mr. Dixon was indeed leaving.

"No one knows except Reese, but he wouldn't tell," said Pru.

"Daddy," Flora whispered. They all looked from one to another. No one said a word, not even Jesse. It was true that Daddy had run off again without a word of goodbye, but would he really report them to Mr. Dixon and have them put in foster homes?

Jesse paced back and forth from the kitchen to the front door. "We have to get out of here," he said to Pru. "We'll take the money Mama left us and go away. Reese will help."

"We can't!" cried Pru as a cold round stone of dread formed in her chest.

"Of course we can," said Jesse. "We have to pack our things. Come on! " Jesse began to hurry up the stairs, with Davey and Flora following at his heels.

"No!" shouted Pru. "We can't! The money's gone! All of it! Every last penny."

"What do you mean the money's gone?" Jesse stopped dead in his tracks.

Pru had hoped she wouldn't have to tell Jesse, that she could put the money back bit by bit, save it up the same way Mama had.

"After Daddy left," said Pru, her heart feeling as though it had dropped off the ends of the earth. She really didn't want to tell Jesse this part. She swallowed. "I looked and the money was gone."

Chapter Twelve

The next to come was the law. They came before the dusk, before the final shades of twilight floundered, before the Burbidges had time to devise a plan.

The sunset was as red as the nightshade berries Pru had picked one day while in the woods. She had planned to eat them—they were such a lovely translucent red, tiny and round and so inviting to look at. But when Mama had seen what she was holding, she'd knocked them from her hand and they had scattered to the ground. "Those plants are poison," Mama had said sternly, "deadly poison." This had given Pru an odd feeling inside.

It was with that very same odd feeling that Pru now gazed at the sun and wished she could put it in her pocket for safekeeping, for if she had things her way the sun would not set this evening. Something ominous was awaiting them in the dark; Pru could feel it in her bones.

Pru had a good view of the hill from the window in the living room. They had been expecting this ever since Mr. Dixon left, so it came as no real surprise when a car popped up over the hill.

"They're coming," Pru called. "The law's coming and there's another car behind them. It's Mr. Dixon's car. Mr. Dixon's with them!" The tires crackled on the gravel stones as the police car came slowly to a stop. The white lettering on the side of the vehicle said "RCMP."

Pru sent Flora and Davey up to hide in the cubby at the top of the stairs, telling them to stay where they were no matter what. She did not wish to alarm them, but at the same time she needed to ensure that they understood the seriousness of the situation. There was no telling what was about to happen now that the law was here. She knew something the law did not: her older brother would not give up without a fight.

Pru glanced over at Jesse. He looked determined, more determined than she had ever seen.

Mr. Dixon hadn't wasted any time. He must have sent for the police right after he left. Pru had not thought the law would come this quickly; she thought that perhaps she and Jesse would have several hours to devise some sort of plan. But with the money gone, there was nothing they could really do anyway. They were trapped with no place to turn, just like that poor little porcupine sitting in the apple tree the day Jesse shot it.

"I could sneak out the back, go get Reese. He might know what to do," said Pru. There was hope in her voice.

"We can't. It wouldn't be fair. If they find out that Reese

knew about Mama he might go to jail. We've got to handle this on our own," Jesse said quite firmly.

"But how?" came Pru's reply as two policemen stepped out of the car.

"I knew he'd call in the law," said Jesse with loathing as he moved the curtain to one side. "I hope he's happy."

"Mr. Dixon's just doing his job," Pru said, watching a look of what she believed to be pure hatred spread across her brother's face.

"I meant Daddy," he said with a sneer.

Pru could not think of anything to say. She was just as bewildered by Daddy's behaviour as Jesse and could not imagine why he would have called in the law. It broke her heart to think he could do such a mean and horrible thing to them. It was bad enough that he had taken their money and left them without a word. But this? What would he have to gain by reporting them to the authorities? Had they not proven they were capable of looking after themselves? And hadn't Mama prepared them for most anything that might arise? Then of course there was always Reese to fall back on if need be. Mama had always said that Reese was the best friend they had.

Pru studied the police officers from this distance. They stood by the roadside speaking with Mr. Dixon and adjusting their revolvers. Mr. Dixon's arms were flying madly in the air, up and down, over and across. *If only I could turn myself into a little bird,* thought Pru. *I could sit in a tree beside them and hear what they are saying to one another.*

Jesse paced back and forth by the window. He had a lot on his mind. His feet slapped against the floorboards; his brow knitted tightly.

"They're coming!" cried Pru as two police officers proceeded toward the house with Mr. Dixon in hot pursuit. In desperation she looked toward Jesse for the answer. He was the oldest, after all, even though they had promised they would make all the decisions together. "They're getting closer!"

Should they run and hide in the cubby with Flora and Davey, hoping they would not be discovered? But surely the police would turn the house upside down and eventually discover them crouched beneath the attic steps.

Jesse gave no indication of what he was thinking. He was standing by the front door now, almost as though he had nothing on his mind at all. Pru could hear the policemen's footsteps closing in on them, the sound of ground thumping with each step they took. One…two…three… four. Closer and closer. They did not appear to be hurried in their steps. Instead, they advanced toward the house as if they had come for a casual visit. When she heard their boots hit the bottom step, Pru looked to Jesse.

"What do we do?"

"Get the shotgun!" Jesse cried out.

The moment those words came out of Jesse's mouth two things happened: Pru ran for the closet to get Daddy's shotgun and the police officers reached for their revolvers and darted behind the woodshed.

Chapter Thirteen

"We just want to talk. Nothing else. You don't want anyone to get hurt, son!" shouted one of the police officers.

"Stay away!" came Jesse's reply. "Stay away or I'll shoot!"

"Listen, son, you don't want to start shooting. You're in enough trouble as it is."

"This is crazy," said Pru as she watched Jesse check to make sure there was a load of shot in the gun. This had turned into a game of cops and robbers, only somehow they were on the wrong side of things and it most surely wasn't a game by any stretch of the imagination. It was real life. Her life—hers and Jesse's and Flora's and Davey's—and it wasn't supposed to be this way. Not this way at all.

"Please, Jesse," she implored. "Someone could get hurt."

"We've got to show them we mean business, that we're not just a bunch of dumb kids they can push around," he said, opening the door a small crack.

As Jesse raised the shotgun, pointing it toward the sky,

Pru raced to the bottom of the stairs. She had to warn Flora and Davey. They would be frightened by the loud noise that was about to follow.

"Stand back!" she heard Jesse call out at the officers.

"Flora, Davey! Don't be scared. It will be loud," Pru called up to her siblings just moments before the shotgun blast echoed inside the walls of the house.

Pru could not imagine a sound being so deafening. It was as if a mighty explosion had erupted right inside the house, causing it to vibrate. The walls and windows rattled from the strain of the blast. A cloud of gunpowder drifted in the air, filling the entire room with its overpowering odour. Hands over her ears, Pru ran to the front door, where Jesse stood braced against the wall, panting from fear or excitement—she wasn't quite sure.

"Are you all right?" she called out, her ears still ringing from the effects of the blast.

"Don't worry about me," Jesse yelled back.

She went for the window and opened it, hoping the smell would escape, waving her hands wildly in an attempt to hurry it on its way.

"Go away," Jesse called out to the police. "Leave us be."

Pru feared then that the police might storm the house, break down the door and start shooting. What would they care about the four of them? Even Daddy didn't care enough to say goodbye when he left, surely some strangers would be no different. Would they all soon be dead, lying beneath the ground with Mama? Pru slid to the floor. Jesse joined her and they sat side by side, their shoulders touching, Jesse with the shotgun clutched tightly in his hands.

"We just want to talk," a policeman shouted back. But Jesse was not about to give up without a fight; Pru could see that all too clearly. This was his home, his family, and no one could have worked any harder over the past months than Jesse to keep it that way. They had both made promises to Mama, and a promise was a promise no matter what the consequence. They would show a united front, just the way Mama had wanted. Pru didn't like it, but it had to be that way.

"It's too late to talk," shouted Jesse. "Now back off or I'll fire again."

"Do you have any more shells?" Pru whispered.

Jesse shook his head. "Reese was supposed to pick some up the next time he got to town."

From where Pru and Jesse were sitting they had a clear view of the road in front of the house and all the area in between. It would be nearly impossible for someone to ambush them through the back door without them seeing. All the same, Jesse got up and barricaded the back door while Pru kept a lookout. She could hear the table being pushed across the kitchen floor, followed by the tall narrow cupboard next to the sink that held Mama's cup towels in the small shelves at the top and her pots and pans in the bottom. She heard the clinking of pots and pans as the cupboard was dragged across the floor and pushed against the door. The last thing she heard was a muffled cry coming from upstairs.

❈ ❈ ❈

Davey was crouched beside Flora with his arm around her shoulder when Pru opened the door to the cubby. As soon as Flora looked up and saw Pru she ran toward her sister's open arms and hugged her so tight that Pru could scarcely catch her breath.

"I told her not to be scared, just like you said, Pru. But it didn't work," said Davey apologetically.

"That's okay," said Pru, holding Flora to her chest. "Sometimes we all get scared."

"What happened, Pru?" asked Flora. "Did Jesse shoot another porcupine?"

"He was just shooting in the air," Pru replied.

"Like when he shot the porcupine?" asked Flora, pouting.

"A bit like that, only nothing died or fell out a tree."

"Can we come down now?" asked Davey. "It's dark in here."

"And it stinks like mouldy bread," added Flora.

Pru could not say no, not with the both of them standing there with the most pitiful looks on their faces. Of course they were frightened. Why wouldn't they be? She was frightened and was most certain that Jesse was too. "You can come down, but you have to be very quiet," she said. "The law is outside the door."

"Do they want to take us away?" asked Davey, his brown eyes widening.

Pru nodded.

Chapter Fourteen

There was something different about Mama that last night and sometimes I think I should have known. But what you really know and what you just think you know are two different things.

We ate supper around five thirty. Even though Mama didn't come to the table those days she came out that evening and sat in her usual place with her robe wrapped around her, the bow tied and slightly off to one side. You could see the material was all bunched up in front on account of the weight she'd lost. When she reached across the table for a cracker, the sight of her thin blue wrists startled me. I closed my eyes and thought instead of the evening Reese ate supper with us and how Mama had sat in that very same spot wearing that very same robe and how Reese had blushed over Mama's thanking him again and again for helping Jesse cut up the maple tree. It was easy to see that Reese felt something special for Mama, and I think maybe she felt the same way too.

※ ※ ※

We ate the last of the cucumbers from the garden that

night. I had picked them two weeks earlier because they were becoming too large. They were big and seedy, as it was late in the season, but it would have been too much of a waste to toss them away. I sliced them thin and sprinkled them with table salt and set a plate on top. I knew they would have little taste but at least we had some new potatoes to go with them. I put a small round rock on top of the cucumbers for a press, one that Jesse had discovered and brought home to be washed in case it was needed. He had intended it to be put on a crock of beans to keep them beneath the brine, but the beans hadn't done as well as we'd hoped and so there was only one crock down in the cellar for the winter ahead.

It would have been nice to have an onion to slice up to go with the meal but I'd used the last one when I'd fried up some deer steaks the previous week because Jesse was awfully fond of fried deer meat and onions. Although I called the dish cucumbers and cream when Jesse asked what we were having, it wasn't really cream at all, but a can of condensed milk that I'd found under the cupboard. I'd added some sugar and a little bit of vinegar, some salt and a little pepper, and Mama had smiled and said I knew as much about cooking as she did.

"Tonight we'll celebrate your cooking skills, Pru," Mama had said, but that usual spark in her voice at the mention of a celebration wasn't there.

"Tonight?" I'd asked in surprise. We could all tell that Mama looked extra tired. She had spent most of the day asleep in her bed and had not stirred even when Flora had crawled up in bed beside her to take a nap. When I had looked in and seen the two of them sleeping so peacefully I'd wished I'd had a camera so I could snap their photograph. Then I'd become upset thinking about how we didn't even have one photograph of Mama, not even a small blurry one. Whatever would we do to remember her once she was gone? I'd wished then that I had taken the money Mama had showed me and bought a Brownie camera, one with a flash to take photographs indoors. And I'd wished I had used up an entire roll of film snapping all sorts of photographs with Mama in them, but you only think of things when it's too late to change them and Mama would have growled that I wasted the money anyway, even though it ended up not doing us a lick of good in the long run. But then we wouldn't have known any of that.

※ ※ ※

Jesse told Mama she should lie on her bed while we dressed up to entertain her, but she said no. "Just play a little music and dance or sing," she said. Although we did as Mama asked, our hearts were not in it. We knew her strength was low even though she tried to put on a brave front. When one of her nosebleeds started, Jesse ran for a cloth. Not until she'd held her head back for several minutes did it stop, and for a time I'd feared it might not stop at all.

"Look at the mess I made," she said, holding the bloody rag in her hand, attempting to smile at the same time. Flora and Davey ran to her and buried their faces in her robe. Mama shushed them and said they shouldn't be sad. Jesse and I helped her back into her bed and when I went to take the pink slippers from her feet she asked me not to.

"I'd like to lay here and look at them awhile," she said.

We all huddled on the bed beside her and talked about our many celebrations. Mama told Jesse and me how proud she was of us, how good she felt knowing that we'd do a good job looking after Flora and Davey once she was gone.

"For the longest time I waited for Tom to come but now I know he won't," said Mama. "Sometimes you have to prove what you can do all on your own without help from anyone."

Mama went on to say how she had thought once about hiring Reese to take her to Annapolis, but that she couldn't bear the thought that Tom might turn her away. "If only he had answered my letter," she said.

"We'll make out fine, Mama. We're better off without Uncle Tom," said Jesse with a confidence in his voice that made me a believer. There had been so many changes in Jesse this past year that I hardly recognized him anymore.

"You shouldn't think badly of Tom," Mama said, shaking her head. "None of what happened in the past had anything to do with you."

"A man's actions speak for him," said Jesse without accusation, and I thought he sounded most grown-up. "Uncle Tom took Nanny Gordon's house from you. He even cut his trigger finger off to get out of going to war. That's the coward's way. Just ask anyone."

Mama reached out for Jesse's hand. "Jesse," she said quietly, "it was Harvey Greer. Harvey's the one who chopped Tom's finger off, fixing up some pussy willows when they were boys."

"But Daddy said…"

Mama made for Jesse to be quiet. "Daddy sometimes twisted the truth, especially when he was angry," she said. "Hurts can run deep. I guess there just wasn't any way to make this one right.

"Your father wanted that house more than I did. He planted the idea in his own head. He fed it and watered it and it grew into something he couldn't control. He thought he could dream it into being his and I was a fool for going along with it. But he knew better—we both did. The boy always inherits the homestead. That's just the way it is. But dreams are what tell us we're alive. Sometimes you just need to have a dream, some way to keep you going."

I caught Jesse's glance. There was no denying the look

on his face—thin lines of doubt were rising to the surface. All this time we'd believed the worst about Uncle Tom. I thought about the day Jesse had burned the letter Mama wrote to Uncle Tom and wondered if Jesse felt remorse over what he'd done. Perhaps Uncle Tom wouldn't have answered Mama's letter, but that was something we'd never know the answer to.

※ ※ ※

When Mama was ready to settle down for the night, she asked me to make some tea using the dried plant leaves she had in the dresser drawer where she kept the money. I made the tea and then right afterward I thought maybe I shouldn't have. But Mama said not to worry because she knew the time was right and that was what mattered. She said the cold weather was coming. So she drank her tea and asked me to go and I did what she wanted. *I only did what she wanted.*

"Some things are best done sooner than later," she said

Chapter Fifteen

Pru forced herself to remain awake even though it was late. She looked long and hard out the window. The near-full moon gave the illusion of daylight outside, but it was close to one o'clock in the morning and a far cry from daylight. She wondered what difference the dawning of a new day would make to their situation.

There were only three candles in the drawer and the lamp hadn't had any kerosene since winter. Pru had lit the first candle as soon as the dusk came and placed it in the middle of the floor. They'd sat around cross-legged on the floor while Jesse had kept watch for any movement outside. Shadows were cast about the room as the darkness had settled in for the night and Flora had been frightened until Pru had showed her how to make shadow puppets of a dog and a bird on the wall with her hands.

Now Flora was curled up alongside Pru, sleeping, and Davey was lying on the floor, his legs tangled into a tight ball, his hands folded with his head resting on them. *How peaceful they look*, thought Pru. It was Jesse's turn to sleep now. He was propped up against the chesterfield in an uncomfortable-looking position with the shotgun lying across his lap. Pru had promised she'd keep the first watch, as she hadn't felt at all sleepy and her mind was filled with all the things she imagined might happen to them. All she could think of was protecting her family and keeping them from harm's way.

※ ※ ※

Things quieted down outside just before dark. The police officers returned to their car to sit and wait and Mr. Dixon positioned himself in the back seat of their cruiser. Davey asked what would happen next, but neither Jesse nor Pru could answer his question.

"Don't let the law take us away," Flora said, looking up at Jesse with tears in her eyes.

Jesse rubbed the top of Flora's head. "Don't you worry. I'll think of something."

As much as she wanted to believe it, Pru was not at all sure that Jesse would be able to think up a plan to get them out of this mess.

※ ※ ※

Pru feared the candles would not last the night and was almost certain they wouldn't until something Mama had shown her came into her mind. Careful not to make any noise and wake her brothers and sister, she lit another candle and went to the kitchen to get the lard kettle. Pru scooped up some of the lard and placed it in a saucer then added a strip off one of the cup towels, leaving a portion of the cotton rag sticking out for a wick. She did the same with another saucer, pleased that she was able to remember so many of the things Mama had shown her before she died. When Pru came back to the living room, Jesse was wide awake, looking at her.

"Where did you go?" he whispered.

"To make some light," she said. "The candles won't last all night."

"You should have woken me," he scolded. "You can't go running off like that. I didn't know what to think."

Jesse lit the makeshift candles and although they did not give off a great deal of light they still helped illuminate the room. Pru could see that Jesse was pleased with what she'd done, even though he did not give her any words of praise. They spent the remainder of the night listening to the sounds of the after hours, the peepers and crickets and a lone bird whose song seemed out of place in the middle of the night. Still, it chirruped with self-confidence, a sweet melodic tune, as if it did not know that night had fallen.

Pru must have dozed off, for she was suddenly wakened by the sound of car doors slamming. Sunlight was extending its slender fingers into every corner of the living room, filling it with a soft radiance. Pru saw Jesse standing at the window with the shotgun still clutched in his hands.

"They're on their way," he said, moving toward the

door. He positioned one hand on the latch and held the other fast to the shotgun. He opened the door a crack and a small stream of fresh air blew into the living room.

"I've got a whole box of shells. Don't come any closer or I'll shoot us. I'll shoot us all! Do you want some kids' blood on your hands?" Jesse's voice echoed loud in the clean morning air. The policemen looked at each other.

"Don't do anything you'll regret, son," one police officer hollered out. "We want to get your brother and sisters out safe. We'll back off. Just don't shoot."

Pru pulled on Jesse's arm, desperation threatening to overpower her. They couldn't just sit there and wait for the police to come in shooting. They had to do something. Surely there was some way out of this.

Jesse closed the door and turned back toward Pru. "What are we going to do?" he asked.

"Tell them we'll talk to Reese Buchanan. If anyone can get us out of this, Reese can. Please, Jesse, someone could get hurt. We can't just sit here forever. We've got no other choice," implored Pru. Jesse pondered her suggestion for a few moments before nodding in agreement.

Opening the door a small crack, Jesse took a deep breath. "Bring us Reese Buchanan."

"Reese Buchanan?" one of the officers shouted in a questioning tone, as if he was confused over Jesse's sudden demand.

"Just do it!" shouted Jesse through the crack in the door. "We won't talk to no one but Reese."

"Fine, we'll bring Reese Buchanan," came the reply. Relief washed over Pru.

"Mr. Dixon's leaving. He must be going for Reese," said Jesse. There was hope in his voice.

Then from the floor came Flora's soft sobs. She sat hunched into a ball with her face buried into her hands. "Is Jesse going to kill us?" she managed to ask Pru.

"Jesse wouldn't hurt a hair on your pretty little head," Pru said. "But the police don't know that. He's just trying to make them go away. See, they're leaving." Pru collected Flora in her arms and stroked her hair the way she'd seen Mama do countless times.

"That's right," Davey cooed. "He's just telling the police that. It's like pretend."

"I wish he wouldn't pretend," Flora sniffed. "It's scary."

"We're all scared," said Pru, wishing that this nightmare was over, that they were out pulling weeds in the garden, just like before Mr. Dixon showed up at their door.

"They're going back to their car," Jesse announced, as if it was his job to keep them all informed as to every movement, every activity from outside.

※ ※ ※

"Pru, I'm hungry," Flora said, tugging on her sister's dress.

Pru sliced some bread, spread it with a layer of lard, and

then sprinkled it with salt the way they did before Mama started getting her welfare check. There was little else she could make without a fire to cook it, and there was no wood in the woodbox since Jesse only brought in enough wood for cooking these warm June days. Pru set the plate of bread on the floor and three sets of fingers each grabbed a slice. The remaining piece was intended for Pru, but she did not think she could manage to force it down, even though her stomach ached with hunger. *If only Mama was here, she'd know what to do*, Pru thought. But if Mama was here they wouldn't have been in this mess in the first place.

"What does that busybody want?" asked Jesse as Mrs. McFarland arrived. She marched past the police officers and stood halfway between the house and the road.

"Pru...Pru Burbidge! This is Emily McFarland," came Mrs. McFarland's sharp voice. "Come out of the house this instant!" She waited for a response. "You don't want to be breaking the law. Just come out and we'll settle this thing once and for all."

Pru did not know what to say and so she said nothing. Receiving no response, Mrs. McFarland turned and walked back to where the policemen and Mr. Dixon were standing. Every so often Pru could hear Mrs. McFarland's voice strike a loud cord. She was upset and excited, as Pru could well make out, even though she could not hear exactly what Mrs. McFarland was saying. Finally Mrs.

McFarland marched out to the clearing again, resting her hands on her plump, oversized hips.

"Pru and Jesse Burbidge, I command you to come out!" she shouted, waving her hands in the air. Her order, however, was met with more silence.

Command! Pru might have laughed were it not for the gravity of the situation they were in. Just where did Mrs. McFarland think she got off by commanding anything of her? Pru was not some genie who had been rubbed from a lamp to grant her three wishes, and were she to listen to anybody in this world it most certainly wouldn't be Emily McFarland.

Mrs. McFarland continued to coax the children from the house using any means she could think of. She promised treats and a hot meal, even a slab of chocolate cake that she said she would produce the second they came out. Finally, in one last-ditch effort, she started marching toward the house yelling out that their mother, God rest her soul, would not approve of such actions. She kept going on until one of the police offers ran out and all but dragged her back to the police car. He opened the door and made for Mrs. McFarland to go sit in the car. After she got in, he closed the door behind her.

"That's one out of the way," said Jesse with a small laugh that angered Pru.

"This isn't a game, Jesse," she said in a serious tone.

Chapter Sixteen

"He's here!" Jesse shouted as Reese's car pulled up beside the road. There was no mistaking the sound of relief in his voice. Davey and Flora flocked to the window. Although Jesse sounded excited to see their old friend, a part of Pru wondered what difference Reese's presence might make. Still, she had to admit it was good to know that there was someone out there on their side.

"He's talking to the police. I wonder what he's saying?" said Davey.

"He's probably giving them what for," said Jesse.

"Now he's coming toward the house," said Davey, motioning for Pru to come look as well.

"Will Reese help us?" Flora asked. Pru could not give her an answer. Would Reese be able to help them, indeed? As Pru watched him close in on the house, that slight limp of his fairly noticeable even from a distance, she felt a surge of hope. About ten feet from the doorstep, Reese stopped and called out to Jesse. Pru tried to run out the door and tell Reese to fix all this, but Jesse caught her and held her fast so that she was not able to break away.

"No, Pru!" Jesse whispered. "We wait to see what he has to say. This could be a trap."

A trap? *Reese wouldn't do anything to trap us,* she wanted to say. "But it's Reese," she said instead, hoping Jesse would come to his senses.

"He could be the enemy," said Jesse.

Enemy? Had Jesse lost his mind?

"It's time you came out, Jesse," said Reese, more serious now than Pru had ever heard him before. "You might just as well know you can't beat the law."

"They'll take us away!" yelled Jesse, opening the door a crack.

"Come out and we'll talk. See what they have to say. I don't want any of you getting hurt." Pru could not see Reese through the small crack but welcomed the familiar sound of his voice.

"No!" came Jesse's cold reply.

"Reese?" Flora moved toward the door and spoke through the small space.

"Yes, Flora?" Reese moved a bit closer to the house and bent forward so that he could hear Flora's small voice.

"Are you going to help us?"

"You bet."

"And Reese?"

"Yes, Flora?"

"The bread's all gone and we're hungry."

"I'll get you something to eat," said Reese.

"Promise?" asked Flora

"Promise…and Jesse," Reese's voice became hushed.

This time Jesse moved toward the open crack. "What is it, Reese?"

"I'll get some food first. Things will look better on a full stomach. Then we'll figure something out. We're going to make this better somehow."

❄ ❄ ❄

In less than half an hour Reese returned with a plate of sandwiches and a jug of milk. He set the food outside the door while the policemen watched. Jesse opened the door only far enough to allow himself access to the food.

"You've got to come out sooner or later, Jesse," Reese said the moment Jesse open the door. "We'll work something out."

"They'll send us to foster homes and you know it," said Jesse, biting into a sandwich. Pru passed the sandwiches to Flora and Davey. Each of them grabbed one off the plate. She took one for herself, knowing she'd have to force it down to keep up her strength if for no other reason.

"I know you don't have any more shells, Jesse," Reese said finally.

"Are you going to tell them?"

Reese let out a sigh. "I don't know. I just don't know," he said, pulling his fingers through his hair. Pru could see the anguish on Reese's face. It was obvious to her that he was struggling between doing what was right by the law and what was right by them. It wasn't fair for them to expect Reese to get them out of this jam. After all, he wasn't even family. He was their neighbour and trusted friend, but still it wasn't fair.

"What about Uncle Tom?" Pru whispered to Jesse. "What about Uncle Tom?" she repeated, shouting it out for Reese to hear.

Pru knew Jesse would be against asking Uncle Tom for his help, but Mama was right, none of what had happened with Uncle Tom in the past had anything to do with Jesse. Like it or not, she couldn't let Jesse's pride get in the way of a peaceful resolution.

"No!" barked Jesse. "We don't need his help. Besides, he doesn't even know us. Why would he want to help after all the things Daddy said to him?"

"We've got to do something. Do you think the police are just going to forget about us?" implored Pru. "Look, Jesse, you never gave Uncle Tom a chance. You burned the letter Mama wrote. People can't help if they don't know."

"Fine then!" let out Jesse, banging his fist several times into the wall as he stepped back from the door.

"Jesse, we have no other choice," said Pru, trying to console her brother. "At least it's something. Maybe he won't come, but at least we will have tried."

Pru looked out at Reese and said, "I think it's our only chance. At least he's family. They might listen to him."

"I think you're right," agreed Reese. Jesse remained silent while Pru and Reese discussed what would happen next.

"I'll tell you what," said Reese finally. "I'll go to Annapolis, see if I can persuade Tom to come."

"I still don't like it," interrupted Jesse.

"Have you got a better idea?" Pru asked. Jesse just shook his head.

"Now, it's going to take me a while to get down there and back," Reese continued. "While I'm gone, Jesse, I don't want you to try anything. Just stay put. I'll tell the police the same. You all just wait. And Jesse, I'm counting on you to keep everyone safe."

"I understand," said Jesse grimly, as if he'd been given instructions on some life and death situation, which might very well have been the case. For the first time since their ordeal began, Pru could see some resolution in sight.

※ ※ ※

The morning dragged into afternoon. Pru set all her hopes and expectations on Reese's return. In fact, she centred her mind on seeing his car come down over the hill. But where was he? Why was it taking him so long to return? Perhaps Jesse was right that Uncle Tom wouldn't help.

Pru tried not to let her apprehension show. It would

only cause the younger ones to worry. She had to be as strong as Gran Hannah, just like she'd been when Mama was sick.

Davey and Flora complained of boredom until Pru interested them in a game of go fish. "I've never played cards on the floor before," said Davey, as if he'd been allotted some grand privilege.

"It won't hurt this once," said Pru, shuffling the deck. She passed the cards around and set the pack in the middle of the floor between the three of them. It was difficult to concentrate on the game and Pru would get up every so often to look out the window. Even with the distraction of playing cards, Flora and Davey grew impatient.

"How long do we have to stay in here?" Davey asked.

"We're waiting for Reese to come back," was all Pru could say.

Chapter Seventeen

Then came the reverend, wearing his white collar. Along with him were the neighbours from down the road and a bunch of people Pru did not know. The sun had crossed the sky. Soon it would be nearing suppertime.

"God is with you," the reverend called out, kissing the cross he wore around his neck on a chain. "I will pray for your safety." Pru could see him inviting a small group of people to one side. She saw them bow their heads. *This can't be good*, she thought, not when the minister is called in to say prayers.

Mr. Hurley, who owned the general store, walked out of the crowd holding out a small brown paper bag and called out to them, "Come out for a candy." People began to gather on the near side of the maple trees, and as the afternoon went by more continued to arrive. Every so often someone from the crowd would shout out to Pru or Jesse, thinking he or she might be able to lure them out. While some came and left, others remained.

"They must think we're a bunch of stupid kids," said Jesse. "But we're not giving up that easy. We'll show them who's boss."

Pru became more uneasy. How would they ever get themselves out of this? She could not tell Jesse that if he had not been there she would have surrendered long before this; she would have run out the moment she saw Reese Buchanan's car pull up.

As it neared time for supper, Flora and Davey began complaining of hunger once again. The sandwiches Reese had brought earlier were long gone. There was nothing else in the house to be had that didn't require cooking.

"I don't have anything to give them," Pru told Jesse, looking at him in hope that he would know what to do. "We'll starve," she said. Flora began to whine.

"We're not going to starve," Jesse said matter-of-factly. "You don't starve in a few hours. Aren't there any preserves in the cellar?"

Of course! Pru had completely forgotten. There was applesauce and some blueberries and maybe even a few jars of rhubarb sauce, all things that Pru had sealed away in jars last year. "Jesse, you're a genius!" she exclaimed, hurrying toward the kitchen.

※ ※ ※

Pru stood above the hatch leading down cellar. It was darker than night down there, cold and damp even during the middle of summer. The air was heavy and stale and the cellar was most surely home to any number of spiders and bugs. But as unpleasant as the cellar was, it was a necessity. It served the purpose of keeping their food cool, especially during the warmer months.

On one wall of the cellar were shelves that held the preserves Pru had put down last year, and in one spot a large flat stone was set into the dirt floor—this was where they placed their pickled beans and cucumbers. One area of the cellar was only partially dug out, and this was where the potatoes were stored over winter. The cool damp earth kept them crisp long into spring. Sometimes when the fall rains came, the cellar would flood, and so several layers of old boards had been placed on the floor over the years to keep things dry. The boards had been lying there for so long that they had begun to decay and this added to the already damp, musty smell.

Pru pulled up on the old leather strap until the hatch opened up. She propped the pole up to keep it open. She was as frightened of knocking the pole down on her way out and getting hit in the head with the hatch as she was of climbing down into the pitch-black cellar. Choosing her footing carefully, she stepped down the steep, narrow stairway, which was little more than a ladder. Mama had always urged caution whenever one of them went into the cellar for something.

Making it to the bottom of the steps, Pru waited for her eyes to adjust to the dim light. She didn't want to make a mad dash and trip over an empty crock, even though she was anxious to get the preserves and crawl back out into the light of the kitchen.

Certain of the cobwebs that clung to the ceiling, Pru tried not to think about the spiders crouched deep into the corners of the cellar, ready to spring upon some unsuspecting prey. Her greatest fear, however, was the discovery of a mouse—or even worse, a rat—scurrying along one of the beams or on the floor by her feet. She knew there were mice in the house. She'd seen their droppings in the pantry and some nights she could hear the distinct sounds of something gnawing. When that happened, she would fling the blankets up over her head to keep out the sound. Jesse had set a trap in the cellar a week before, but it was empty and sitting next to the wall. A shudder passed through Pru as she continued her way to the preserves, using the light from the open hatch to see her way to the shelf.

Above her, Pru could hear Jesse's voice. He was talking to Davey and Flora, ordering them to listen was more like it. Jesse said he didn't like them running through the house unsupervised, not with the law outside their door. He thought they should sit in the living room and be quiet, but Pru knew better. Davey and Flora were too young to remain seated for long. It was hard enough getting them to sit still in school, let alone expecting them to do the same at home. When she heard the sound of little feet running across the floor, Pru figured Jesse had finally given in and allowed Davey and Flora to run free, something they'd been moaning to do for hours.

Finally the shelves came into focus. Pru was surprised at how many full jars were still lined up on the shelf. She usually sent Jesse or Davey down to the cellar when she needed something—they didn't seem to mind climbing down into a mouse-infested dungeon. They had all worked so hard last year at picking berries and tending to the vegetable garden. Last spring when he was cleaning out his own cellar, Reese had given them his mother's mason jars to use to preserve their harvest, and there had also been some in the house when they'd moved in.

Mama had stressed the importance of preserving berries when they were in season. "Nothing will taste better than blueberries or strawberries in the dead of winter," she had said. Well, this wasn't the dead of winter, but Pru had no doubts that they would taste just as good. Unable to distinguish what was in the jars, Pru chose two from the shelf.

As she turned back toward the steps, Pru heard a tremendous crash up above her. What sounded like a stampede of footsteps stormed across the floor. This was followed by a knocking and banging that seemed to shake the entire house.

"Hurry up, Pru!" she heard Davey's voice echoing down into the cellar.

"What is it?" she cried. "What's going on?"

"They're at the back door!" came the reply. "They're trying to break it down!"

Pru could hear someone trying repeatedly to get into the house, with little success. Jesse had barricaded the door shut. But what if they succeeded in breaking it down? She could hear Jesse calling out and he sounded angry.

"I'm going to start shooting!" she heard Jesse shout.

Panic ripped through the fabric of Pru's being. With a swift movement her imagination leaped into places so dark and frightening that she could scarcely catch her breath. Another crash followed.

This time Pru was immersed in total blackness.

Chapter Eighteen

I screamed for Davey to open the hatch. I wasn't even sure if he could open it, as heavy as it was. The darkness was all-consuming. A crushing fear curled up inside me and wouldn't leave. I had no idea which way to turn. More muffled sounds came from above, along with the occasional thump and the clump, clump, clumping of feet. Then I heard Flora's long drawn-out scream and it nearly caused my heart to grow cold. Something had happened, something horrible. Flora needed me. Jesse and Davey needed me. They all needed me. The sound of feet running across the floor above me gave way to a feeling of sudden and desperate urgency. I had to get out!

I could hear Flora crying and I knew Jesse would not know how to make her stop. I had done it so many times after Mama died, when Flora would wake in the night sobbing uncontrollably. But Jesse did not know any of this. He did not know the special noise I made to quiet Flora or the way to get Flora's mind off what was troubling her. He did not have my tender touch.

I could hear Davey yelling from the other side of the hatch. "Pull it up!" I shouted.

"The strap broke. I can't open it. I'm trying, Pru. I'm trying!" came Davey's muffled cry.

I couldn't just stand there in the dark. I had to get out. But which way should I go? Little steps or big steps? *Think, Pru, think.* But it was as difficult to think as it was to breathe. The darkness began to close in around me, as if a heavy cloak of doom had settled on my shoulders. I knew I had to move, but I was afraid of the very act of moving in complete darkness. If I could just make it to the hatch, I could help push it open. Closing my eyes, I tried to envision the cellar, picturing where the preserve shelf stood, where the earthenware crocks were sitting, where the steps leading out would be. Tears stung the corners of my eyes and my chest ached as I let out two quick gasps, determined not to cry. Never in my life would I have imagined such total and utter darkness. *Think, Pru, think.* But the only thought that came to my mind in that moment was that "If only..." game we used to play with Mama.

"If only I had some light," I whispered, hoping by some miracle that my wishes would turn into reality. And wouldn't that be the simplest thing in the world? But things are never that simple and I knew it. I had gone over that fact many times while Mama was sick.

I could hear Flora's muffled wailing from up above as her screams turned into tears. Desperate to help, I took a small step forward, knowing I had to do something. Sliding my feet along the bottom of the cellar, I felt my way along. *Easy does it.* Another step and another and I felt my foot touch the decomposed boards on the cellar floor. I was making progress. I could still hear Davey struggling to open the hatch.

"If only I had some light," I said again, this time louder to give myself courage. I thought about how courageous Mama had been all the while she was sick. Hearing my voice so loud and strong filled me with a renewed sense of optimism. I would make it out one way or another. I had to.

Then I thought I heard someone call my name. I stopped in my tracks and listened.

"Pru...Pru."

"Who's there?" I asked, feeling my body trembling.

"I'm here beside you," the voice whispered, filling the darkness with a melodic vibration that hummed like the strings of a violin. This time there was no mistaking it. I felt my knees go weak and nearly dropped the jars of preserves.

"Mama!" I gasped. "Is it you, Mama? Are you here?" It *was* Mama's voice in the dark with me. It had to be. And yet it couldn't be. I waited for a reply but none came. Still, I hadn't been mistaken. I'd heard a voice and the voice was Mama's and she was calling my name.

"Do you remember our day in the woods, Pru—just you and me?"

"Yes, Mama, I remember."

I closed my eyes and thought of the day Mama and I had gone to search for gold thread. I remembered the peaceful feeling that had come over me while we stood listening to the sounds all around us. I quieted my breathing and thought on it with everything I had. I remembered how Mama had asked me that day if I could feel Gran Hannah's strength and wisdom and how uncertain I had been at the time. As I stood in the dark with my eyelids clenched tight, concentrating on that day, I felt a warm hand touch my cheek, a touch so soft that it sent a shiver down my spine. I realized in that moment that I was no longer afraid.

"You can trust Uncle Tom. I want you to tell Jesse it's okay to trust Uncle Tom," came a soft whisper.

Suddenly, a fracture of light entered the darkness as the hatch door opened. "I got it!" cried Davey.

"Mama…Mama," I whispered, but there was no reply. It was as if a bubble had just burst; the magic that Mama's voice had brought was suddenly gone.

"I'm coming, Davey. I'm on my way," I called out as I etched my way toward daylight.

When I emerged from the cellar I found Jesse in the living room, Flora cradled in his arms. Flora was sobbing quietly. Davey was bouncing around looking as though he didn't know what to do.

Jesse looked up and saw me standing in the doorway. "What took you so long?" he asked.

"I'll tell you later," I promised, knowing there was no time to go into details now.

"Pru!" Flora cried out the moment she saw me. She wiggled out of Jesse's arms and began to hobble her way across the room. I ran to meet her and in one swift movement swept her off the floor and into my arms.

"Let's see what happened to you."

"The step, Flora went though that rickety step," said Jesse, sounding full of disgust. "I knew we couldn't trust the police to wait for Reese. They tried to break down the back door and now Flora's gone and busted her foot." How could so much have happened in those few short minutes when I was in the cellar getting preserves? I set Flora on the chesterfield.

"Now close your eyes and make a wish," I said, slowly removing Flora's stocking. Flora did as she was told, but the moment I began to remove the stocking she winced. "Oops, it came off," I said, waving the stocking in front of Flora. "You must have made the right wish."

I asked Jesse to get a wet cloth. The only thing I could do to help Flora's foot was apply a cold compress. I hoped the well water would be cold enough to do the trick—it was all we had. I could hear Jesse working the handle of the pump up and down, and then a steady stream of water coming out of the pump.

I looked down at Flora. "See now, we'll patch you up better than new," I said and the smile returned to her face.

"I didn't mean to break the step, but the police were trying to get in and Jesse said for us to hide and then he said he'd shoot if they didn't go," she said. "And Pru?"

"Yes, Flora."

"I wished for the step to be fixed."

"Don't worry about that silly step," I assured her. "It needs to be replaced anyway." Poor Flora, if only things were as easy to fix as that broken step would be. Again I wondered just how this would come out in the end.

I placed the cold cloth on Flora's ankle. "We could really use some yarrow about now," I said.

"Like the day Mama hurt herself on the step?" asked Flora. How surprised I was that Flora had remembered the day Mama had sent me out to pick yarrow.

"That's right, Flora. Yarrow!" I said happily. "It's a treatment for bruises and swelling. I thought I forgot but I remembered! And there's juniper gum, for cuts and sores; burdock, for stomach ailments; and gold thread too." I kissed Flora on the top of her head, thrilled that she had suddenly jogged my memory. It was all coming back, all the things Mama had told me about the plants on our outings in the woods, the things that Gran Hannah had passed on to her. Mama was right; I could feel Gran Hannah's wisdom. It was somewhere deep inside me, along with her secrets. Now I know what Mama meant.

Chapter Nineteen

Pru spooned the blueberry preserves into four bowls and passed them around. She could not imagine being trapped inside the house much longer, especially not with everyone on the outside coaxing and pleading for them to come out and thinking that Jesse might do something so silly as to shoot at them. Only they didn't know Jesse. They all thought they did—the policemen who pulled out their guns and made ready to shoot, the minister who prayed for them, the neighbours who had hardly bothered to say hello whenever they saw Jesse at Hurley's store. Not even Mrs. McFarland. Especially not Mrs. McFarland. Jesse was no danger to any of them and yet they did not see it that way.

Both Davey and Flora were filled with questions as to why Reese hadn't returned, and Davey began to state the things that Reese would do once he finally came back, as if Reese possessed some special powers to make everything better. Davey ended it with, "When Reese brings Uncle Tom back they'll both show them."

"Maybe Uncle Tom won't come," said Flora, sounding depressed at the thought.

Pru watched Jesse scrape the last of the blueberries from his bowl. She knew he still wasn't pleased at the thought that they had to ask Uncle Tom for help.

"We'll see once Reese gets back," said Jesse, sounding quite pessimistic.

"You don't think Uncle Tom will come, do you?" asked Pru.

"He might, and then he might not," said Jesse. Standing, he moved back toward the window and pulled the curtain aside.

Pru gathered up the blueberry-stained bowls and took them into the kitchen. She did not bother to wash them, as there seemed no point in it. For a time she stood by the sink holding the dirty bowls and recalling what had happened earlier when she was trapped in the cellar. She thought once again about the day Mama had taken her out into the woods and how Mama had said she could sometimes hear Gran Hannah's voice and feel her touch. Was it really Mama she'd heard down in the cellar or had she just conjured the words she thought Mama might say in her head? It was difficult to say. Should she tell Jesse what had happened? Or would he just laugh? As she set the dishes in the sink she heard Jesse anxiously calling for her.

"It's Reese's car coming over the hill!" cried Jesse. Davey and Flora were standing in front of Jesse, clapping their hands and jumping up and down. Pru hurried to look out the window. Sure enough, down the hill came Reese's green Chevrolet.

"Did he bring Uncle Tom?" asked Flora.

"There's somebody in the car with him!" exclaimed Pru as she watched Reese's car slow down. Surely it was Uncle Tom. Reese had come through for them again; he'd convinced Uncle Tom to come help!

Reese parked his Chevrolet in front of the black and white RCMP car and jumped out. He said a few words to the policemen and then motioned for the person in his car to get out. The Burbidges all stood at the window waiting to see what was about to take place. It seemed to Pru as she watched the two men approach that everything was happening in slow motion. Reese led the way, followed by the passenger of the car, and behind them the two policemen. The curious onlookers moved slowly forward, as if they were realizing that something pivotal was about to take place and were afraid they might be left out.

When Reese and the others got halfway to the house, one of the policemen spoke. "Are you willing to talk, Jesse?" he asked.

Jesse did not move right away but stood as if frozen in one place. He looked at Pru and nodded gravely then looked down at Davey and Flora. They were looking up at him with anxious expressions. Jesse moved toward the front door and opened it a crack.

"What do you want?" he called out.

"Will you talk to Reese Buchanan?" asked the police officer.

Just then Reese took a few steps forward. "We need to end this, Jesse," he said.

"What's he want?" asked Jesse, motioning toward the man who arrived with Reese.

Stepping out in plain view, the man called out, "It's Tom, your Uncle Tom. I'm here to help. I know you don't know me, but Issy was my sister. Family has to stick together."

"Yeah, well you should have thought about that before you stole Nanny Gordon's house away from us!" shouted Jesse, slamming the door shut, his face flushed red with anger.

He looked at Pru. "I think this is a mistake. He can't do anything. He'll just mess things up and they'll still send us away."

"Uncle Tom wouldn't be here if he didn't plan to help," said Pru, her heart thumping madly. She couldn't let their only chance of getting out of this mess slip away.

"But he stole Nanny Gordon's house out from under us," said Jesse.

"You're all the family I got," Uncle Tom called out. "Family has to stick together." He began walking slowly toward the house.

Jesse opened the door up a crack. "Maybe it's too late to be looking for your family, mister. Don't come any closer or I'll shoot," he warned. Uncle Tom stopped in his tracks.

"Reese knows we have no shells, Jesse. There's no point in keeping this going. We can't stay in here forever," whispered Pru.

Jesse stood shaking his head. Davey went to say something and Jesse told him to be quiet. "We've got to talk this out, Pru. I still don't think he can be trusted…"

"Don't come any closer," repeated Jesse, turning his attention back to what was going on outside the door.

"Jesse," said Pru, looking her brother directly in the eyes. "When I was down in the cellar…" She swallowed hard. She had to tell him what had happened. One way or another, she had to make him understand. "When I was down in the cellar I heard Mama's voice." A dazed look spread across Jesse's face.

Pru placed her hands on her brother's shoulders. It had been a tiring ordeal, one that needed to come to a conclusion. Pru could sense a change in the atmosphere. This might very well be her last chance to make Jesse understand. "Jesse, Mama said I should tell you to trust Uncle Tom."

"Mama? You heard Mama?"

This time Jesse did not argue.

Chapter Twenty

It is a long way to drive in the heat and a long time for Flora and Davey to sit still. Uncle Tom has already stopped the car once because Davey was car sick and he says it's a good thing we don't make this trip every week. Before we left we packed a picnic lunch of potato salad, fried chicken, and chocolate cake and set it in a basket. We even took plates and mugs and some forks and knives from home because we knew it would be an all-day trip. I didn't put any frosting on the cake because Uncle Tom said it would melt in the heat and end up smeared all over everything. Davey moaned on account of there being no frosting and Jesse told him not to act as though it was the end of the world.

Jesse and I are sitting in the back seat. I can tell Jesse doesn't want to miss a thing, the way he's sitting with his head turned toward the window. Sometimes Uncle Tom calls out about something he sees along the way. Then Jesse and I grab fast to the back of the front seat and try to get as close to the windshield as possible.

Uncle Tom says it's only right that we visit Mama at least once or twice a year. Today is our first visit since we left last summer and moved in with Uncle Tom in Nanny Gordon's house.

The policemen took Jesse with them that day at the house. Jesse held his head high when he walked past the group of onlookers, unashamed of the way he had fought to protect us all. I was proud of the way both Reese and Uncle Tom stood up for Jesse, telling the police that we'd only just lost our mother a few months back and were still in shock over her death. Uncle Tom told them they should be glad that there had been a peaceful resolution and that no one was injured. When the policemen said we had unlawfully buried Mama, Jesse told them that we'd laid Mama to rest in the cemetery outback. Reese spoke to the fact that the old cemetery would be considered a proper burial ground and to prove it he told Jesse to take them out and show them where the other tombstones were.

"There wasn't but the one shell in the entire house and Jesse only shot that as a warning," I heard Reese tell them.

They turned the house upside down that day and even searched Jesse's pockets, but of course they couldn't find a single shell. They didn't think to look in the damp dark cellar, and I'm not sure they would have found anything even if they had—it's too dark down there to see something as small as a shotgun shell lying on the floor. Jesse doesn't know that when I took the gun from the closet and slammed the door it caused a shell to fall off the shelf. Jesse thought there was only one shell, the one that was in the gun. But there was another one, which I slipped into my dress pocket before I handed Jesse the gun. I can't explain why I hid the truth from Jesse, but something told me it was right. When the police tried to break down the door, I pulled the shell from my pocket and threw it over my shoulder.

I don't know how they did it, but Reese and Uncle Tom finally talked the police out of pressing any charges, although now someone from the Children's Aid drops by the house once a month to make sure we're staying out of trouble. Uncle Tom always laughs when they leave and says, "They just want to see if I'm feeding you."

It turns out that it was that busybody Mrs. McFarland who told Mr. Dixon about our situation. It seems that her husband saw Daddy in Bridgewater, buying himself a train ticket. Daddy was never one to keep things to himself, so it was no surprise to learn that Mr. McFarland had overheard Daddy telling someone that Mama had died recently.

We haven't seen Daddy, not since the day he left. I think Mama was right, though; Daddy is a restless spirit, one who may never settle down. Knowing that doesn't stop Flora from crying out for Daddy in her sleep, but time has a way of easing the hurt and it been months now since Flora woke in the night.

※ ※ ※

Our first stop is to visit with Reese Buchanan. When we pull up, Reese is working in his woodpile. Davey and Flora bolt from the car and run toward him. The moment Reese sees who it is, he throws down his axe and drops to one knee. Davey and Flora climb all over him, laughing and squealing with excitement. I see a flicker of sadness in Reese's eyes even though I can tell he is putting on a brave face. I am sure he has missed us this past year as much as we've missed him.

"Look how you've all grown," says Reese. He tousles Jesse's hair and Jesse gives him a playful nudge. "Pru, you're a young lady now. And Miss Flora, who stole your front teeth?" he asks. Flora gives a wide-angled smile and says they fell out on their own.

"If this keeps up you'll have to get yourself a set of those false ones like the old folks wear," says Reese, and it sends Flora into a fit of laughter.

Uncle Tom has brought his camera and we stand in front of the lilac bush to have our picture snapped with Reese. The sun is over Uncle Tom's shoulder and it shines directly in our faces, but it is the only way to take a picture outdoors and have it turn out properly.

Uncle Tom surprised us one day with pictures of Mama, pictures that Nanny Gordon took when Mama and Uncle Tom were growing up. There's one of Mama in pigtails, wearing a million dollar smile and a pretty cotton dress, sitting beside a lake with Uncle Tom. There's even one of Mama and Gran Hannah.

"See the devil in Gran Hannah's eye?" laughed Uncle Tom when he showed me. "You never knew what she was up to."

My favourite picture of Mama was taken on her wedding day. She and Daddy are standing in front of Nanny Gordon's house. Mama is holding a bouquet of wildflowers and there's a rose tucked in her hair. They both look happy. I try and imagine myself in the past, looking on as Nanny Gordon would have when she took the picture, but it is impossible. I see the look of hope in Mama's eyes, feel the promise so deep in her soul, and see her whole life spread before her. Knowing as I do the way it all would end I have to stop myself from crying.

We take our picnic lunch to Torment Lake and spread a blanket on the beach. Reese did not want to come, but Uncle Tom insisted. By the look on Reese's face I think now that he is glad he came. He's at the water's edge, pant legs rolled to his knees. Jesse and Flora and Davey are all trying to coax him into the water. But he is not getting wet, he says.

A gentle breeze is blowing across the lake. It blows the hair from around my face as I stand high on a rock overlooking the water and watch some loons bobbing in the waves. They do not appear to notice anyone in the water with them and continue their journey toward the shoreline. They dive below the water and come up not far from where Jesse is swimming. The moment Jesse sees the loons he swims out to meet them, his arms beating madly on the water. Again they slip below the surface and disappear. Jesse stops to see where they will break surface.

We eat our lunch on the beach. Reese and Uncle Tom rave on about my cooking and I know my face is red. I tell them it's only potato salad and chicken and that anyone who can read can follow a recipe. Uncle Tom laughs and says he's gained ten pounds since we came to live with him.

After lunch, we drop Reese off at his house and go farther down the road to visit with Mama. I don't tell anyone about the many times I've seen Mama in the dark. I take my turn standing by the white cross Reese made to mark Mama's grave. We all lay down flowers and then we tell Uncle Tom about the celebration of the pink slippers and about the parade we dressed up for. We tell him about the "If only..." game we used to play and Jesse tells him we don't have to play it anymore. We talk about the times Mama took us to the woods with her to look for plants and berries.

"Issy always liked the woods," says Uncle Tom. "She spent hours there with Gran Hannah."

I do not tell Uncle Tom that I already know these things, nor do I tell him that I have seen the glint in Gran

Hannah's eyes and her soft puckered smile. I do not tell him that I have felt her small warm hand slip inside mine as she stands on my right and Mama on my left. And he would surely not understand our many adventures deep in the woodlands of Nova Scotia.

※ ※ ※

At night I close my eyes and travel back to the Dalhousie Road. I wait for a few moments and before I know it I am stepping over the threshold of the house we once lived in, the house Daddy promised he'd buy for Mama, only he ended up leaving us all behind. When Mama comes out to meet me she is pretty and plump just the way Nanny Gordon liked. There is not even the slightest sign of sickness on her face. She is wearing the pink slippers Flora and I bought at the rummage sale and she grabs my hand and we run off toward the woods in search of plants. Mama goes over them all with me, pointing out each plant and its uses. She shows me leaves and berries and I listen as closely as I can to pull her sweet voice across time. When Mama can't remember the name of a plant or bush, Gran Hannah is never far away.

※ ※ ※

During the day when I am not at school I write it all down, all the things Mama and Gran Hannah show me. Last week Uncle Tom brought home a plant book from the library and I looked up deadly nightshade and copied the important parts from the book down in my pages:

Nightshade or Bittersweet: This plant is sometimes called "deadly nightshade" because its leaves and unripe fruit contain alkaloid solanine. Some of the symptoms of poisoning include vomiting, thirst, lethargy, and laboured breathing. The toxin is not normally fatal when used for medicinal purposes and the dosages are carefully measured. The berries change from shiny green to bright red. The purple flowers hang down in clusters and each flower has a yellow beak at its center. The Bittersweet plant was used as a charm many years ago in England to counter the effects of magic.

I have underlined the sentence that says the toxin is not normally fatal, even though I sometimes wonder if that would still hold true with Mama being as sick as she was. But I can't let that thought consume me because, like Mama used to say, it's hard enough to live with what is, let alone ignoring what could be.

One day I told Jesse about the tea Mama asked me to make. I knew it was time he heard. He listened while I spoke and did not interrupt.

"You were there when Mama needed you," he said. "You did what she asked and it's okay." I don't know why, but Jesse's words released something inside me. Tears filled my eyes and I felt a great relief.

※ ※ ※

Dusk is settling in as we climb back into the car to begin the long trip back to Annapolis. Flora rests her head against Uncle Tom's shoulder. I hear her yawn and I know that soon she will be fast asleep. We go through The Ridge and follow the narrow winding road shaded by hardwood, travelling up past the Forty-Seven River and over the Camel Hills. It is all so familiar, every turn and dip in the road, for it is the way I travel at night when I'm on my way to visit Mama.

We drive with the windows partway down, a warm July breeze blowing in on us. Before we turn off the dirt road and onto the paved highway to Annapolis, Davey turns around in the front seat and waves goodbye. Jesse and I both turn and watch the dirt road disappear from our sight.

I do not feel as though we are leaving anything behind. It will all be there for us the next time we come through. In the meantime, I have Mama and Gran Hannah to talk to. I know what it is like to visit with the old people, the ones who came before. I have their love and their wisdom, which has been passed down with each generation. The words are all written down on paper now, and they are not just for me and Flora and Davey and Jesse, but for all of those who will come after. This will be our story.

Acknowledgements

My sincere thanks to Caitlin Drake and everyone at
Nimbus, to my family and friends for their words of
encouragement, and to the community of
East Dalhousie, Nova Scotia. Your faithful support
has meant a great deal.

And to Brian; your love and support has meant the most.